THE SAHARA OBSTACLE

BY
OGHENERO JONATHAN EGHWEREE

Embark on a poignant journey across continents in "The Sahara Obstacle," by Oghenero Jonathan Eghweree. With a career rooted in journalism at the Federal Radio Corporation of Nigeria (FRCN), Oghenero brings his expertise to vivid life in this gripping tale. Following his acclaimed work "Muri the Whiz Rat," he delves into the lives of four Nigerians – Daba, D1, Victor and Mena – as they confront daunting challenges in their homeland.

Aided by Jasmine, their friend in Libya, and driven by stifling visa restrictions and a bleak landscape for youth opportunities, the quartet embraces a daring mission: crossing the Sahara Desert. Their destination? North Africa, a gateway to the promised lands of Europe just a perilous stretch away. From the bustling streets of Nigeria to the arid expanses of Niger Republic and the volatile terrain of Libya, their journey unfolds against a backdrop of courage, friendship, and the harsh realities of migration.

"The Sahara Obstacle" is not just a narrative; it's a reflection of our times, exploring themes of love, loyalty, and the profound consequence of chasing dreams across borders. Oghenero captures the emotional turmoil of each character, their aspirations, and the sacrifices made in the pursuit of a brighter future.

As you immerse yourself in this compelling narrative, you'll witness firsthand the triumphs and tribulations of those who dare to defy the odds. Whether you are drawn to tales of resilience, African literature, or the human spirit's indomitable will, "The Sahara Obstacle" promises to captivate and inspire.

Oghenero Jonathan Eghweree, holds a B.A. in International Studies and Diplomacy from the University of Benin, Benin City, Nigeria (2009), and a PGD in Mass Communication from National Open University of Nigeria. His insights as a Principal Reporter|Editor enrich every page of this novel, making it a must read for enthusiasts of contemporary African literature.

This book is dedicated to the families, and to victims who have lost their lives in the Sahara Desert, on the quest to seek greener pastures in Europe.

May their souls rest in peace. Amen.

Published in Nigeria in 2024 by
Delightful Clicks DCStudios WED30042019
23 Mokolo Close, West-End Asaba, Delta State
MOBILE: +234 703 555 3724
EMAIL: info@thesaharaobstacle.com
www.thesaharaobstacle.com

ISBN: 978-978-766-190-1

A catalogue record of this book is available from the National Library of Nigeria.
ISBN: 978-978-766-190-1

TABLE OF CONTENTS

CHAPTER 1

ONE SIDE OF THE COIN

He sat up, and took the remote control on top of the mattress on the bare floor where he has laid, and switched off the 14Inch Sony TV on the wall. The One Bedroom apartment had been serenaded by soft music from the advertisement on the television, but all was quiet now.

The picturesque advert had showed an airline offering to take travelers to the locations of the world's seven wonders. It promises a comfortable travel time, with beautiful airhostesses pampering passengers, with their white teeth in full glare, which had kept DABA spellbound.

He thought about how wonderful it would be to go on a world-wide spin to China, Peru, Mexico and other locations where the wonders are sited.

He was reliving the pictures he saw on SSB moments ago, still stuck in the zone those marketing geniuses have kept him.

Daba adjusted his fully loaded, brown hanging bag, as he stepped out of the apartment, while still buttoning his blue jean jacket. He stopped after completing the first three buttons from the bottom, to leave a good view of his broad chest, and took long strides towards the burst of loud music, from an even louder engine of a car parked in front of the building.

'Dependable D1!' he hailed, as he approached the light green Mercedes 220.

Daba is the leader of a four-man team, all bellow the age of thirty, who are about to embark on a mission to Europe. They intend to get to Libya by road through the Sahara Desert, and then cross the Mediterranean Sea, to Southern Italy.

On the driver's seat of the Mercedes was DAFINONE, or D1, as everyone know him. He has been pumped up for the trip since he finally found someone to sell the car to a fortnight ago, to cover expenses for the adventure. He had almost lost hope of being part of the journey to El Dorado, thus his excitement.

He had sold it to JIMMY ADADA, the Councilor representing his ward in the local government council, for two hundred and fifty thousand naira.

'Dafinone, I will allow you use the car until you travel,' Adada had magnanimously announced before the payment was finalized.

'Bring it to my place the night before you depart,' the potbellied local legislator had told D1.

'Please don't forget to do that before you *jand,*' Adada had emphasized before letting go of his hard-earned cash that day.

The gesture was according to the Counselor, part of his contribution towards assisting D1 in his ambition to travel out of Nigeria.

He had said, 'times are hard, no one else would have doled out that amount of money for the Benz,' as he is wont to call the car.

In Southern Nigeria, "to Jand" means to travel abroad. Likewise, a "*Jandon*" is someone who has embarked on such a trip, or a Nigerian who resides in Europe or America.

To be a *jandon* was the main thing in the 1980s and 1990s. To have one in a family then, was worth bragging about. And many youths in Nigeria, still nurture the dream of relocating to Europe or America.

However, towards the end of the last millennium and the beginning of the twenty first century, this reverence for Nigerians who have traveled abroad, as well as the dream to be like them began to wane. This was due to some social and political changes within and outside the continent.

One of the factors responsible for the change in attitude was the return to democracy in many African countries by the year 2000. The system of government had brought in certain positive structural changes which were only beginning to manifest in countries like Nigeria, Senegal and Ghana, as the millennium progresses.

Conversely, the influx of illegal migrants into Europe and America over the years, had also necessitated the countries who were most affected to come up with stringent immigration laws targeted at Africans, especially Nigerians.

These changes seriously affected many who had illegally crossed over to the West. Some were deported and returned home, broke and hopeless. The situation also made the process of getting visas to western countries difficult for Africans. Thus, migrants resorted to devising any means possible to get to Europe, just like the mission which has been activated by Daba and his crew.

The idea of the journey came about around January 2015, following an infamous boat mishap in the Mediterranean Sea, involving over seven hundred migrants, including women and children. The craft had taken off from a location in Libya, en route Italy. That particular incident had sparked international outcry and put a spotlight on the migration crisis in the Mediterranean region.

The incident was relayed in surplus by local and international news and current affairs outlets across the globe. Daba and VICTOR, his coworker had received the information at the barbing salon one quiet Saturday morning.

The news had come up on AIT News, while they were putting the shop in order, with MENA, Victor's girlfriend seated in front of a mirror at a corner doing her make up. Instinctively both men left what they were doing and fixated their attention on the TV. Daba held tight to the napkin in his hand, while Victor stopped sweeping as they watched with rapt attention.

'Look!

'Germany and Sweden have opened their gates to the migrants.

'Look!' Victor gestured, pointing towards the bottom of the screen where a headline appeared at the red section reading: "GERMANY, SWEDEN ACCEPT SYRIAN MIGRANTS," before the letters escaped into the network trademark, in time for the rest to see what he was talking about.

'*Daba we fit go o*!' Victor enthused in the Nigerian Pidgin English, spoken in many parts of Nigeria and West Africa. He looked at his friend, and then, at his girlfriend and back and forth.

'*Na true o*,' Daba responded calmly.

He was still digesting the magnitude of the crisis and the glaring opportunity which it portends for intending migrants, who could reach the Mediterranean Sea and join the hustle, as his friend had suggested.

'*Make I call JASMINE first*,' he stated in the same manner, as he brought out his phone to dial his longtime friend in Libya.

That was the origin of the expedition as Daba still remembers it. Things have happened so fast in the past months since they got the news that some rich western European countries had opened their gates to migrants. And they had made plans to utilize the window while it lasted. All is now set for the trip to the Northern Nigerian City of Kano, for the first part of their journey.

Daba reflected on these things as they drove through the bustling 242 Road in Oghara, to D1's family compound. He was also seriously bothered about what would become of his mother KIKKI, if anything should happen to him while he was gone. But he felt it was his last chance to take the bull by the horns and take his family out of poverty for good.

'I have to take the trip.' He subconsciously reassured himself, then joined D1 in singing the lyrics of 2Pac and Dre's "How Do You Want It," playing in the car. The sound from the beat reigned in the air as the occupants flowed with the rappers, with the volume at a disturbing level.

Just then, the car pulled off 242 Avenue, into a bumpy road leading to D1's house. Jerking on his seat, Daba searched for his phone in one of the numerous pockets of his ash colored combat short. He brought it out and dialed GYADHI.

Gyadhi is the pick-up guy operating in the Northern fringes of the Sahara desert. Jasmine had appointed him to handle the difficult stretch of the journey from the border between Niger

Republic and Libya, across to Tripoli. But first, they have to play their part by meeting up with the transporter at Al Qatron, where he'll be stationed awaiting their arrival.

MASTER OF THE DESERT, as he was widely known by his peers, Gyaadhi has made over two hundred expeditions across the Sahara Desert, which separated North Africa and Sub-Saharan Africa.

The difficult terrain of the desert has turned a handful of drivers like him, who transport people across it, into highly valued commodity.

LIBYA

After a long listen to a rhythmic Andalusi music Gyadhi used as his call-tune, he took the call and shouted 'hello,' into the mouthpiece of the NOKIA 3310.

'It is me Daba, Jasmine's friend,' the Nigerian caller said at the other end, and waited for a reply from the Libyan transporter. Although they have spoken many times before, yet the man had somehow refused to store his number and had always made him reintroduce himself whenever he
calle

'Ah! Greetings my friend!' fired the usually loud Gyadhi, after recognizing the voice at the other end of the phone.

'Jamin say you people leave your country this week, true?' Gyadhi asked in broken English. It was his best effort to liven up. He would have preferred to maintain a silent gaze on the dusty highway as he drove, rather than have a conversation with a guy he hardly knew on the other side of the Sahara Desert. He had had to take the call though, because it was important; it was Jamin's contact.

'Just checking to know if everything is still according to schedule' Daba continued on the other end.

'We take-off tonight,' he informed the point man in Libya, who in turn assured him that all was in order at his own end of the deal.

'"The Black-Horse," as he calls his truck, 'is ready to take you people to your destination.

'Is that Good?' Gyadhi asked, holding the phone to his mouth and speaking into it like he was using a transistor.

'Good to know,' Daba responded.

'Thank you, Gyadhi,' he said, and ended the call.

At that point the Benz pulled into "Villa," as D1's house is popularly called. Victor and Mena were on the veranda cuddled, as they rested on their own hanging bags, while facing the road.

D1's house was not a villa in the real sense of the word, but was referred to as such, because it was the name giving to the building by his father.

It even carried the inscription "VILLA," at the front of the house, close to the roof.

The three-bedroom flat, with two separate bedrooms and an additional two rooms attached to it, was the first of its kind in the locality, when it was built back in the early 1980s. So famous was the structure then that people from nearby villages would come to take a look at the much talked about edifice. Many also use the picturesque Villa, with flowers of varied colors, for their picture stand during holidays like Christmas and Easter celebrations. Although, by the late 1990s, a few modern houses have begun to spring up in the area, thereby diminishing the fame of the Villa. Yet, its popularity endured, and it remained a notable landmark in Oghara.

D1's mother was the eldest wife in the polygamous setting, and she occupied a room in the main flat referred to as her "Gate". It was there that D1 and his friends had converged on for their departure night.

An hour after the crew arrived at the Villa, D1's mama, with her large frame stormed the crowded room where they were gathered shouting, 'oya, oya, oya o!' She used the popular Yoruba parlance to spur them to gather at a small table in the middle of the room to have their diner. Between her two large hands was a stainless steel tray full of rice, with spoons pierced into it from all sides, and having abundant stew on top of it like icing on a cake.

'D1, oya, come and eat.'

'Daba!' She said loudly, 'oya, come.'

'You two,' she gestured towards Victor and Mena, using her head to direct them to the center table where she had placed the pile of rice, with four medium pieces of meat. They all gathered and pulled spoons out of the heap of rice, and within minutes, the tray was empty and looking like the arena of a dancing competition between two chickens.

That night as they lay to sleep, cramped in the room. Each of them strengthened their resolve to embark on the long journey to Europe by road, through the Sahara desert, and then across the Mediterranean Sea. The next morning they would travel to nearby Benin City, to commence the journey.

CHAPTER 2

THE FLIP SIDE

Jasmine is the contact person in Libya, assisting the latest group of four immigrants bound for Europe, on their journey to the transit country. Libyans pronounced his name as "*Jamin,*" and he sort of liked it that way. He welcomed anything that would hide his identity in his adopted country.

He was often seen in a *jalabiya* (a long tunic), a *sirwal* (trouser), and a *sadriya* (a vest) embroidered with black silk, with a white cap to match. He liked to dress this way, because he felt it made him look like a typical Libyan. However, many residents especially in the urban areas of the North African country now prefer western clothing like jeans and shirt. Yet, Jasmine has several copies of the same outfit and only dresses differently whilst in his hotel room, or during a nocturnal activity.

He emerged from the driver's seat of the Toyota Land Cruiser that afternoon, with a sense of urgency, and breezed into the elevator on getting to the lobby of the Pyramid. Inside, he hit the square button with the number “10”.

Jasmine had less than an hour to make it to his bank at Tajura, close to the capital city, else he would miss the month’s payment to the special account.

The payment to a savings account in Nigeria, by the 29th of each month, was a top priority for him.

The account belonged to his mother OMATIE, back home in Oghara. Since he left home nine years ago in 2006, Jasmine has not missed a single payment into that account. Not even when he was a wharf rat, with little to feed. Even then, he had managed to send her some money using middlemen. These days, he does the transaction using various methods, all usually initiated by himself.

In the elevator Jasmine reflected on a recent boat mishap in the Mediterranean Sea, where another two hundred black emigrants have drowned, with no survivors. He felt nauseated.

He was pained that despite the experience of many who have lost their lives on the journey across the hot Sahara Desert, and the formidable Mediterranean Sea, yet every year many African youths still trope into North Africa from the southern parts of the continent, on the dangerous quest for a better life in Europe.

'Anyway, I was once naughty like them,' he subconsciously admitted, as he stepped out of the elevator.

The memory of his journey from Benin-city, in Southern Nigeria to Tripoli, was still fresh in his memory. He figured the journey to Europe across the Sahara Desert should be even more difficult these days for the modern African daredevils, due to the ongoing conflict in Libya. He thought that in time past when the rule of law prevailed, even then, the migrant's agents in Libya had succeeded in operating a system which posed a lot of difficulties for the African migrants. Not to talk of now that hell has been let loosed, with the unending conflict. This is coupled with the entry into the thriving migration industry by anyone who own a ferry, and was willing to transport people across the Mediterranean Sea to Europe, at a price.

He went straight to the reception on getting to the tenth-floor, to check for new messages and to relay further instructions to ALICE, the enthusiastic receptionist from Italy.

'Assalamu-alaikum,' Alice greeted in Arabic and beamed as she is wont to do, when Jasmine walked towards her. She sat behind a large desk facing the elevator in the lobby of the exquisite 10th floor of the Pyramid.

'Wa alaikum assalam,' Jasmine responded and received the items stretched before him by the lady who maintained her grin.

'You had two calls, one from Nigeria and KHARIG called as well. He said you should meet him at the Spotlight, tonight. That he has got something which requires your urgent attention,' Alice reeled in seconds.

'And Omon is inside waiting for you.' She concluded.

Jasmine thanked her and headed straight for Suite 69.

Alice has become like a personal secretary to Jasmine, since he chose the Pyramid as his base, after joining the Clique some years ago.

The receptionist too has been there that long. The place has been a base from whence Jasmine crisscrossed the length and breadth of the country doing his thing.

'Things hardly change in this highly coded, but popular five-star hotel in the heart of Tripoli,' Jasmine said, as he rounded off his thought and tapped on the golden plate on the door with the label "S69". He knocked on the door with the palm of his left hand, while using his phone to dial Omon's line with his right hand at the same time. He now had about forty-five minutes to get to the bank for the "Special Transaction" and time was of the essence.

Omon opened the door after a few taps, and gave him the stare.

'Always in a hurry,' she said and walked across to the sofa to resume her movie. She continued to talk about how her day was boring, as Jasmine absentmindedly rushed to the bathroom to have a quick shower.

He returned to Omon a few minutes later looking crisp, with a small bottle of the Hugo Boss perfume in his hand. With a romantic grin, he took few neat sprays on his replaced *jalabiya*, kissed her on the lips, before zooming out of the room.

Omon had been distracted from Bruce Willis's "Hustle in A Good Day to Die Hard," and had kept a fixed gaze on Jasmine, until he left the room. As he shut the door she reflected on Jasmine's rapid growth in Tripoli and how he has become a big shot in the Clique right before her eyes. She was proud of him for what he had been able to achieve in the city, despite having a rocky start in the country.

However, his rise to prominence in the organization has not come without its challenges for their relationship; such as Jasmine not spending enough time with her, as she would have loved. The situation has become worse, after she quitted her job at the club for him. But she was learning to cope with it nevertheless, due to the love she has developed for him over the years.

After over eight years together, she has come to understand his every move: the good, the bad, and the hustle, and she loved him all the same.

She knew from their first encounter at the underworld night-club in downtown Tripoli that the guy had baggage, but fell for him not because of his stunning looks, but for his bravery.

It had all happened when jasmine was about getting his feet on the ground in Libya. That day Omon was carrying an innocent face, which made Jasmine wonder what she was doing on the pole, at the secret nightclub inside the Spotlight. So enchanted was the African migrant at her beauty that he stood up for her, when some men tried to mess with Omon on stage. Of course, the guys were as carried away as he was, so a brawl broke out which left Jasmine with a cut on his face, before he was thrown out of the hotel by some mean looking guys. They had spared him, because he had a valid pass into the club in the first place.

It was Jasmine's first time at the Spotlight on special invitation by a stranger he had met earlier in the afternoon, at the Tripoli port. It was the invitation he had mentioned that gave him security clearance into the hotel and the secret section he was directed to, where he met Omon.

As he dusted himself to leave, Jasmine heard a whisper from one of the side-doors of the building. The place was not as bright as the main entrance, but Jasmine was able to identify the caller by her curvy shape, which was now engrained in his memory in only a short time. It was the enchantress.

'Am Omon,' she said, stretching out her hand, as she came out of the shadows.

'Am Jasmine,' he replied, taking her hand.

'Do you want help with that?' she asked politely, pointing to the thin cut on his fore-head.

'Am ok,' Jasmine feigned toughness, trying to maintain the macho act. Although, at the back of his mind, he wondered what prompted him to get involved in the fight in the first place. Normally he'd look away in such situations, but there was something about her that made him lose his cool, when the two drunken, rich-looking men climbed her stage and started fondling her, despite her mild resistance.

Omon moved even closer and said, 'thank you,' with a little smile that blew Jasmine off his feet, into a wonderland full of exciting twists and turns.

He was only disrupted from his reverie when a stocky fellow, with a demeanor of sophistication, beckoned him over, accompanied by two huge men.

It wasn't the Briton Jasmine had come to see. Nonetheless, he got his first assignment from the heavily built man who said his name was Kharig. From then on, his fortunes in Tripoli had transformed for good.

***

INTERPOL HQ – Lyon, France

7.50am

'Gentlemen, thank you for being here on short notice for this brief, but all-important meeting, before our Global Conference commences in an hour's time.' President of INTERPOL, LEON WERNER, said to three, out of the thirteen members of the Executive Committee of the International Criminal Police Organization, who had occupied the chairs facing him.

'I believe you have all been following the news about the escalating migration crises in North Africa.' Leon spoke in English tainted by a strong German accent, as he branched into the agenda of the meeting.

'Please, take a look at page 11 of the dossier in front of you,' he gestured to the others using his own.

'Our sources say another boat carrying over two hundred emigrants capsized last night, near the Mediterranean island of Sardinia in Italy, none survived.' PETE ARNOLD, the Head of North American regional bureau of INTERPOL said solemnly, after seeing the pictures and data on the page.

'Over eight thousand people, including women and children have perished in like manner this year alone,' Leon picks up from where Pete stopped.

'What about our investigation into the criminal activities of the Clique,' the INTERPOL President inquired from the African Bureau Chief, DAYO OLUSOLA.

'The 2011 SACK MIGRANT'S AGENTS, SMA mission has been greatly affected by the crises in Libya, which is the hub for emigrants crossing to Europe, but we have finally made a headway.

'Special Agent JAKE THOMAS, has identified a key suspect in the organization. We are onto him.' Dayo stated.

'We must escalate our activities in Libya,' MILANO BELLUCCI, the INTERPOL European regional representative from Italy contributed, due to the implication of the crises for his country, rather than his best professional assessment of the situation.

'We must allocate more resources towards eradicating the activities of migrant's agents in North Africa, before things gets out of hand.' He said, out of frustration.

'Well, we will find out about that today at our congress,' Leon interjected.

'Gentlemen, take a critical look at the dossier and suggest workable recommendations before the week runs out.

'We must indeed, do something urgently. And we also have a conference to attend,' he added, on a lighter note, then stood up to shake their hands as they left.

***

Jasmine got to Tajura at 1.30pm and parked at his usual spot by a Chinese restaurant, opposite his favorite bank branch. After about five minutes in the car studying the environment from his side and rear view mirrors, he stepped out and took a short walk into the Oriental Continental Bank for the special transaction.

By 1.50 pm, he had made the payment, and was heading to his car, but still felt something was not right.

'Those weirdoes at the counter,' he said, reflecting on the strange behavior of two young men he noticed at either side of him when he collected the teller from the cashier before leaving the bank. He was troubled whether it was a coincidence that they had arrived the bank almost at the same time with him, and the two of them departed just as he was about to leave.

Smugglers are prone to paranoia just like other criminals, and they hated coincidences.

Jasmine's case was especially so, because he held the RECO badge in the smuggling ring known as the Clique. The RECO badge was held by those known as the Recommended. It was a status attained in the organization after a member was recommended for the position by another RECO fellow, to become part of the leading echelon of the Clique. The recommender of the Recommended is also known as the Linksman, which in Jasmine's case was Kharig.

There are different levels of influence among members of the nocturnal body: the Eyes on the streets, the Executioners, the Recommended and finally, the Head, the elusive Briton.

Jasmine had been one of the most successful Executioners for the Clique, with many important missions accomplished before his elevation. He was also until recently, the coordinator of all the migrants' agents working for the Clique, before the organization diversified into other more lucrative, illegal businesses.

His current project was a personal one though. He had made arrangements for four of his friends in Nigeria to join him in Tripoli, where he had also made plans for their immediate transition to Germany, via Italy, which was just across the Mediterranean Sea.

Inside the car he repeated the routine with the mirrors, and for a moment forgot about the scare from the boys earlier. He then gave Gyadhi a call to confirm the extant arrangements.

Gyadhi answered the call after the first ring, and assured Jasmine, saying, 'Don't worry, everything is in place to get the crew to you as planned,' he emphasized.

'Don't worry!' he reechoed, before Jasmine hit the red button on his phone screen.

He had parked the vehicle along a row of cars by the busy Ed Dachla road, in the northern part of Tajura. And now, he thought the road was hyper busy, with unusual number of people at the sidewalk. He took a quick look around before sliding into the road and drove away slowly. He was yet to recover from the possibility that he was being followed, after the incident at the bank.

'These four will be my last.' Jasmine soliloquized inside the SUV, as he exited the long road after about ten minutes' drive.

He connected the Tajura-Tripoli highway, and increased acceleration. The thought of the strange boys never left his mind throughout the course of the drive back to Tripoli.

CHAPTER 3

THE CREW

It was as if the British abandoned three wives, some concubines and their children, leaving them to fend for themselves on October 1st 1960, when Nigeria attained independence. Moreover, the freedom agitators at the time felt there was no better time for the people to govern themselves, but as soon as possible.

Unfortunately, in less than a decade after independence the country was bedeviled by coups and counter coups, and eventually a civil war in 1967. The situation led to a gradual decay of many basic institutions, and the little infrastructure the colonialists had left behind. By the 1980s and early 1990s the highly endowed country began to experience signs of economic difficulties and an increasing unemployment rate.

The youths were the most affected by the aftermath of the national tragedies, especially from the 1980s onward. This was due to the fact that there were only several active policies by successive governments, aimed at improving the lot of young people throughout that period.

Matters were made even worse by the quality of graduates produced from the decaying and ill-equipped tertiary institutions in the country. The universities and polytechnics were riddled with corrupt lecturers who accepted bribes from male students for grades, and demanded sex from female students to pass exams.

Moreover, a good percentage of students in the campuses were either preoccupied with other negative, extra curricula activities like cultism and prostitution, while others were hooked on drugs and gambling. Education for many of them was a formality, while to *jand* was the ultimate dream of young Nigerians. The trend has continued even after the new millennium.

The four young Nigerians: Daba, Victor, Mena and D1 are all products of the system. They are all graduates without meaningful skills for long term sustenance. Each of them had a story which bothered on the situation in the country, except Mena.

Mena was from a rich home. Her father MR ADEKOKO, owned successful businesses in Lagos, and other major cities in Nigeria. She opted to be part of the trip because she did not want to be separated from Victor, her lover. They have been together since their second year in the university and there was no end in sight for their relationship, despite Mr. Adekoko's staunch disapproval of their union.

Victor on the other hand, was a multi-talented young man in his mid-twenties. He had been the best in class, with a steady 4.7 GPA in his university days. He was also well known throughout the Faculty of Arts, at the University of Benin for his charm and genius. However, his poor background had been a hindrance that his academic fame and physique could not make up for, then, and now.

Back then at campus he was often seen begging for fifty naira here and a hundred naira there, which did a lot of damage to his image, but many still respected him because of his brilliance. Although he put in long hours doing menial jobs at Daba and Jasmine's saloon and completed assignments for lazy students in the faculty, it still wasn't enough to maintain a decent living, let alone cover expenses such as buying books and paying school fees.

However, his fortunes would change on one of those difficult days in school. It was a Friday, after a long lecture on an empty stomach. He stepped out of the lecture hall and leaned on the rays barricading the third floor of the faculty of Arts building, and wondered where his next meal would come from.

Suddenly, an aura from behind caught his attention. He turned to behold an overdressed girl standing right next to him, with a condescending look.

Victor glanced at her briefly, before returning to leaning the top half of his body on the rail, his gaze fixed on activities on the ground floor of the building. He left the position after a while and faced Mena who was still standing there, and crossed his arm to wait for what the affluent looking girl had to say. The girl was famous for her flashy looks in campus, but Victor was not in the mood for what was not profitable at the moment.

'Hello, how are you, Victor?' Mena asked, standing close to him with a big, black leather bag on one hand, and a Blackberry Z10 smart phone on the other.

'Yes.' Victor managed to reply through a wrenched stomach.

'How may I help you?' he asked.

'I want you to do a school work for me,' Mena spitted out bluntly, without changing her posture and acted in a manner that was almost offensive. But somehow Victor kept his cool and focused on the opportunity for a meal, which had just presented itself.

'Who told you I undertake projects for people?' he asked, trying to feign not-too-willing. Doing what Nigerians call '*sakara*' in local parlance.

‘Are you doing it, or not?’ Mena demanded, still keeping the posture and the attitude, like she was annoying Victor on purpose.

‘I’ll give you N1000 naira upfront, as half payment. I will pay the balance on completion of the work by Monday, if you agree.’ She said.

Mena then reached for her bag, not minding the obvious look of astonishment on Victor’s face, brought out two pieces of N500 notes and stretched it towards him.

Victor snatched the money from her hand without any attempt to hide his desperation and ran towards the stairway.

After a few steps in the descending direction, he climbed back again, and ran to where Mena was still standing, albeit dumbfounded. He took her phone and hurriedly typed his number. He returned the phone to her and dashed off again, this time shouting, ‘text me the question!’ As he ran down the stairs towards the school canteen.

***

At 8 a.m. on Monday morning Mena was already at Victor’s hostel called “Black Gate,” located off campus, and was banging on the gate like there was trouble.

The hostel was called Black Gate for two reasons: it has a huge black gate, and most of the boys in the hostel are members of one of the dominant fraternity in the school known as “The Axe-men,” with black, as their favorite color.

So when she came banging at their gate that early in the morning, the inhabitants did not find the disturbance funny. And it took the quick intervention of Victor's roommate D1, who horridly came out to bail the situation.

As soon as Victor managed to get Mena into the single room he shared with Dafinone, he grabbed her shoulders, and shouted, 'what is wrong with you! I shouldn't have texted you my address, you busybody!' He yelled out of frustration, before letting her go. He reached for his bag on top of the small wardrobe, in the small room where they kept most of their stuff, brought out the work and handed it to Mena.

'Please, leave!' he said and gestured towards the door and refused to accept the balance of payment Mena was offering apologetically.

He saw her off and ignored her when she tried to offer further apologies.

Victor stood by the gate and watched Mena leave and thought she would have been a sweet girl if not for her brattiness.

At that moment D1 came to where Victor was standing. He noticed the direction of his friend's gaze towards the departing lady and said, '*the chick no bad shaa*!' which in the local Pidgin English meant, the lady was good-looking. He was insensitive to what might have transpired between them. He went on to ask if she gave him the balance payment for the assignment.

'Please tell me you have the money, Victor, am starving!' He said excitedly.

The question annoyed Victor, but he simply ignored Dafinone, and made for the room to avoid an argument with his benefactor. As a squatter in the apartment, he treaded on a thin line and would do everything possible to avoid unnecessary arguments that could provoke his host in school.

CHAPTER 4

THE REST

D1 is a nice guy, who would do anything for his friends, but his flip side is terrible. He could probably be one of the most annoying persons who ever stepped foot on earth, and on this occasion he was at his worst. Coupled with the fact that he was experiencing a downside financially.

One week has passed and he was still nagging Victor about the money he refused to take from Mena.

'That money would have sustained us by now,' he would remind Victor, whenever they were alone in the room, broke and hungry.

'If not for your moment of temporary madness we wouldn't have been in this excruciating situation,' D1 continued to fume on this occasion, as they both lay on the rug with their heads on the mattress, which was also on the floor. The rug and the mattress are the only furniture in the "single-room self-contain," as such accommodations were called.

The room was filled with bags and books. There was also a small gas burner, along with small and medium-sized pots and other utensils arranged in one corner of the room, designated as the kitchen.

Sometimes they entertained guests too, and there could be up to six to eight individuals cramped in the small room.

Victor just laid there with his eyes wide open, gazing at the ceiling, not minding his friend. After almost a year in D1's room in squatting capacity, he has learned to tolerate the negative side of his benevolent host, such as the complaining he was faced with at the moment. In all, D1 has been an angel positioned to help him at a time of critical need.

Dafinone, which was his real name, was shortened to "D1" by his friends, and he was quite popularity back home in Oghara. The name had come about during an era known in the locality as "*Mellina*".

The *Mellina* period in Oghara, coincided with the trend in the 1980s and 1990s, when some of the unemployed youths in the nation have begun to exhibit signs of frustration, leading to high crime rate orchestrated in various forms across the country.

In the northern, eastern, western and southern Nigeria, there were widespread cases of robbery, kidnaping, allegations of ritual killings and other crimes. These were trending delinquencies, before the now blossomed Advance Fee Fraud activities on the internet, known in Nigeria as "*Yahoo-Yahoo,*" *or* "*419*".

'*Mellina,*' was one of such criminal activities common in Oghara during the period. It involved the illegal tapping of rubber trees, at a large rubber plantation owned by an old private firm in the area. The clandestine tapping of rubber by the boys, sometimes men, even women at the farm, nearly caused the collapse of the company.

Dafinone, also known as "Designer-One," was a legend in the trade. He derived the nickname from the notoriously deep cuts he inflicted on the rubber trees he tapped. He always desired maximum bleeding, regardless of the age of the tree, suitability for tapping and overall implication for the plantation.

Up until the late 1990s, rubber was still one of the leading industries in Southern Nigeria, and especially in Oghara town. But the industry began to wane as the new millennium approached. The decline also corresponded with the peak of the *Mellina* era.

The business was lucrative for D1 and his cohorts, who organized themselves into groups to storm the rubber plantation at night. By morning time when the rubber had turned solid, they would sell the produce to agents, who in turn sold to rubber factories for hard cash.

However, with time, the Management of the rubber plantation soon devised stringent security measures to end the *Mellina* trade. While some of the boys got arrested, some others were not so lucky and got themselves maimed with acid and other dangerous weapons deployed by owners of the rubber plantation, in the effort to deter the criminals. These measures contributed to ending the illegal operation, but not before making some of the perpetuators rich including Dafinone.

Although D1 generously spent the proceeds from the *Mellina* crime with friends and family, he never lost sight of the reason he got himself involved in such a dangerous venture, which was to amass enough money to enable him procure a visa to leave the country.

'I have saved up to three hundred thousand naira, mama.' Dafinone proudly announced to his mother one morning, while he was having breakfast on the small table in her Gate.

'Three hundred what?!' She said back, stunned by the amount of money D1 had mentioned.

'Dafe,' she stressed in her special way of calling him, inwardly concerned about the prospects of her son getting into trouble from his dealings.

'What are you going to do with all that money?' she inquired.

'Mama,' D1 responded after swallowing a lump of *garri* he was having with *banga* soup.

'Half of me is already in Europe, while the one you see now is finalizing plans to join him,' he said, and continued molding the next lump of *garri* to go.

'What is the plan?' she asked.

'Am leaving for Lagos, first thing tomorrow morning to see BROTHER WHISKY. He has promised to procure a visa to Holland for me, in just next three weeks.

'Three weeks, mama!' D1 said excitedly.

'Three weeks and all would be set for me to leave, can you believe it!' He animated.

'Wow!' Mama D1 screamed, infected by her son's excitement.

'My son!' She exclaimed, and leaned over to give him a tight hug.

Her actions made the lump of garri D1 was holding in his hand to fall into the plate of soup, and it splattered a few drops of oil on their clothes. She ignored what she had done, got up and started dancing and singing at the same time; '*my son o, my son o, my son o!*'

D1 smiled as he watched his mother dance to the news. He was happy to see her thrilled by his progress and hoped to make her proud someday.

He took a few quick swallows of the *garri*, and ate the piece of meat and fish in the plate. He then grabbed a sachet of water on the table, tore it open with his teeth. After taking a sip, he left the room to hit the streets. All the while his mother was still singing and dancing: '*My son o, my son o.*'

Dafinone travelled to Lagos the next day to see Brother Whisky, an unregistered travel agent and a distant relative who lived in Amsterdam, to complete arrangements for a visa to join him in Europe.

Whisky the Jandon, is a six feet two inches, heavily built man with fair skin. He uses his influence as a jandon to feign expertise as a travel agent, whenever he was in Nigeria for a visit. He capitalized on the ignorance of many of the aspiring jandons, who did not want to approach embassies directly for visas for fear of rejection. This he does for them, mostly by illegal means and in return, collects exorbitant amount of money for travel fees. While some of them luckily succeeded and traveled to Europe, many others were not that fortunate, and that was the case of Definone. Thus, after spending most of the money he had saved during the Mellina venture, he still could not get a visa to travel abroad. Whisky, his supposed agent had returned to Europe without informing him. Even his foreign numbers were no longer connecting, like they used to when he was in the Netherlands.

On the other hand, the plantation where they carried out their illicit activity was undergoing a torrid time and was on the brink of collapse, due to the un-coordinated tapping of the rubber trees. The place was now almost useless, consequently, the situation brought the Mellina business to a complete halt.

After the Mellina era ended, and the incident with Brother Whisky, Daba found coping with life in Oghara unbearable. He struggled with the reality of idle existence which followed the earlier vibrant period of abundance. He had no other savings and no one to depend on.

Although his father MR. OJO, was still alive, Dafinone could not rely on him for anything.

His favorite line when Dafinone asked him for something was, 'I have four wives and twelve other children to cater for, besides you.'

By the age of thirteen, he had ceased asking his father for anything, and had begun supporting himself.

A month after the heartbreak of losing his money to Whisky the Jandon, D1 left home to join his old friends, Daba and Jasmine to hustle in the ancient Benin City, which was 121 km from Oghara .

'I need to chill with you guys for some time,' D1 had said to Jasmine and Daba, even before he stepped a foot into their room at Black Gate. He could be that direct. It was already past 10pm, when they welcomed him to their hostel that night.

'Where are you coming from?' The boys had asked, surprised by his sudden phone call that night that he was already at their gate, before the unexpected request.

Whatever the case may be, they did not turn him down. Dafinone was one of the most enterprising young men back home, and his peers held him in high esteem. Again, their salon in campus could need an extra hand. They thought D1 would also fill in the gap in the event that both Jasmine and Daba had classes to attend within the same time frame. They were also confident of D1's resourcefulness. But he did not join them at the salon.

Instead, in less than a year in Benin City, Dafinone was able to penetrate the used-car sector, and was fast becoming one of the go-to-guys for buyers whose budget could not afford a foreign-used, or a brand new car. He served as the middleman between those who intend to sell their used cars, and the buyers, and gets his commission when the deal is done.

He even retained the room at the Black Gate, with Victor as a constant guest, after Jasmine and Daba left the accommodation for a more befitting place.

Despite the setback from the experience with Brother Whiskey, Dafinone never stopped considering leaving Nigeria, and he was swift to declare his intention to be part of the mission when Daba told him about the plan.

CHAPTER 5

THE CLIQUE

For many decades smugglers and migrant's agents have operated freely in Niger Republic and Libya, except for the payment of little dues here and there to local authorities. This in turn, had granted them the right to do whatever they wanted in the Sahara Desert and environs, and across the Mediterranean coastal cities in the North African country.

Their operations over the years have become more sophisticated, with the entry into the trade by some top dogs in Libya, who had business and political connections in Tripoli.

One of such illegal smuggling ring was the Clique, masterminded by Mifta Rajab.

The Clique is a professional, well financed and structured criminal organization, with different units who function in specialized fields, for the ultimate progress of the group. Their sphere of interest includes: shipping, smuggling, militia activities, hotel operations and prostitution.

The leadership activates any of the specialized units to achieve its objectives, whenever the need arises, and engages them on a contract basis.

The group was formed in the late 1990s by an Englishman from Yorkshire, named John Mountbatten. He had come to Libya as a young freelancer with his friend Harold. They had visited for a journalistic adventure after the hype that followed the September 1, 1969 Revolution in the country.

However, the duo got into trouble in December that year, while pursuing a lead on the activities of an opposition militant group in the Cyrenaica region, at the eastern end of Libya.

Their leader, HAMUZ MOHAMMED and his supporters known as the Redeemers, were ardent followers of the deposed king Idris I, and were opposed to the regime in Libyan, led by Colonel Muammar Gaddafi. Their aim was to overthrow the government, eliminate the leader and reclaim power.

On that fateful day, the Redeemers mistook the journos for government agents and opened fire as their vehicle appeared from a distance at Tobruk. Harold took a bullet to the chest in the rapid firing that followed. He did not make it out of the encounter alive, but John did. He was held hostage by the group and kept under the direct care of Hamuz himself.

The leadership of the Redeemers had dreaded a diplomatic debacle with Britain, whom they hoped would give them diplomatic support and recognition to achieve their aspiration. So all evidence of the accident was erased, and Hamuz Mohammed had John Mountbatten indoctrinated and made a member of his group.

John's enterprise and dedication would endear him to Hamuz, who was at that time, one of the most deadly militant warlords in the Middle East and North Africa.

Aside his determination to excel in the organization, John also displayed organizational skills, and delivered in whatever task he was assigned to execute and often exceeded expectations.

The militant leader later appointed John Mountbatten as his Chief of Protocol, cum Media Strategist, thus making him one of his key aides. He was also converted to Islam, and he adopted the name Mifta Rajab.

Hamuz Mohammed would later meet a tragic end, when he and many of his supporters were ambushed at the graveside of his wife SADIYYA, who had died after a long battle with cancer. He was killed alongside three of his eldest sons, who collected hot bullets from AK47 rifles of government forces, who stormed the scene and opened fire before the grieving recipients could recollect themselves.

The incident led to the total crushing of The Redeemers, because of the enormous influence the charismatic Hamuz Muhammed wielded on the organization.

Mifta Rajab went underground following the death of his mentor, and the final attempt by the regime to crush the group. He had been on the government's wanted list prior to the incident, but efforts to arrest him was accelerated after the demise of his boss.

This was due to the critical functions he had carried out for Hamuz Mohammed personally, and the Redeemers as a group.

How he escaped the onslaught at the Black funeral remains a mystery to those in the Libyan security architecture. Moreover, all his files with the authorities were wiped out following the demise of Moammar Gaddafi in 2011.

Mifta Rajab, now in his sixties, had carried with him to exile, the connections and lessons he inherited from his master. He was one time a major player in the underworld business of smuggling people to Europe, not only from Libya, but across the entire Maghreb region. He had a super influence in cross-border transactions and the regional arms black-market as well.

He had set up the new base of his thriving empire in Egypt, and oftentimes visited Libya to oversee some of his interests in the country. He has done so successfully over the years due to his mastery of the art of disguise and excellent planning skills.

One of his major area of interest these days was is in the shipping industry, with his vessels operating mainly within the Mediterranean Sea. He also manages a freight operation network under the guise of a Swiss conglomerate known as, *La Voyage*.

It was on one of such missions to the Tripoli port, while pretending to be a Canadian businessman that he was stalked by a handsome, but hungry looking African, who repeatedly asked for a job, promising he'd do anything for money.

'Let me by your boy, sir.

'I'll be a strong hand for you.

'I'll do anything,' the boy said repeatedly, sometimes interchanging the sentences.

'I'll do anything.

'I'll be a strong hand for you.

'Let me be your boy sir.' He said again and again, as he followed him.

John lost his patience after several quick steps to evade the determined young man and was on the lookout for a convenient corner to escape. He stopped when he was sure he was out of plain sight to take a good look at the young man who was pestering him.

Upon closer observation he saw that Jasmine was not a lunatic, because he could see the sheer desperation and hunger in his eyes. He also noticed the boy seemed confident, even in his disadvantaged position, and looked ready to face his challenges headlong, and at any cost.

'He just might come in handy,' Mifta Rajab thought, as he studied the youth some more.

'How are you sure I can be of help to you?' the Englishman then asked the young man.

'I know that at least you own this ship' the boy said, pointing to a large ship receiving heavy freight attention with the inscription 'La voyage,' boldly written across it.

'I have been watching you from over there,' Jasmine pointed to another direction where some containers were piled by the roadside. 'My name is Jasmine and I desperately need a job.' He said.

'Meet me at the Spotlight tonight,' Mifta Rajab said. He gave Jasmine a hundred dollar bill and went away without saying another word, leaving the hungry man surprised and filled with joy.

It was a gamble, and Jasmine was happy about the outcome. It has earned him some good money, and an appointment with a very important person. He could not believe his luck.

Jasmine had gone three straight days without food, and was beginning to think he would die of hunger for real, unlike the relatively mild type he had escaped from back home in Nigeria.

The migrant kissed the bill a couple of times and rushed back to the shade under the pile of containers where he had earlier been, to contemplate where the Spotlight was located and how to get there. He had by this time made friends with some die-hard Libyan dock boys or *dock rats,* as they were fondly called, and was sure one of them will have an answer for him.

Meanwhile, all of Jasmine's problems seemed to have vanished. He brought out the dollar bill from his pocket at intervals to take a quick look before carefully returning it with delight.

Jasmine later met Kharig at the Spotlight instead of the Briton himself. His relationship with Mifta Rajab, the boss, has been that way. They mostly communicated through a proxy, with few exceptions.

CHAPTER 6

THE SAHARA OBSTACLE

THE REBIRTH
As the choicest desert Africa
Alas, her remains is like that of an old man;
Feeble and devoid of the zeal of the hay days.
Weaning uncontrollably and heading for the inevitable.
The body is no match for the super viruses of nepotism and corruption,
That plague the homeland,
Beating it to submission.
No youths to stay and lend a helping hand,
They are fleeing the land like one affected by an epidemic.
Perhaps, hope lies in death.
When the circle is complete,
And the westward spin of civilization turns around,
From its westward spin to the east;
And back to Africa.
Then shall the anguish come to an end, and the continent's glory restored.
That time shall surely come,
Because what goes around, comes right back around.
***

Victor ended one of his crazy writings, folded the piece of paper he wrote on neatly and placed it in his breast pocket.

'Earth was designed with strategic borders, or obstacles to deter the easy migration of people from one location to another. Perhaps, to contain humans within their continental divisions,' Victor said, in an attempt to explain their journey to Mena.

'Why this is so remains a mystery just like many of the world's wonders, but they are there: mountains, oceans, rivers, seas and deserts, all there to restrict us to our regional and continental divide.

'We humans have only succeeded in making the movement of people from one geographical location to another a fraction easier with technological inventions such as the internet, airplanes and ships. But the vast majority of people around the world are still permanently put in check by the earth's boundaries. The Sahara Desert is one perfect example,' Victor landed.

Mena was paying attention, as she rested her head on Victor's chest. They were at the back seat of an 18-seater Toyota Haice bus, filled to capacity, under a temperature of 30 degrees Celsius and without an air-conditioning system in the vehicle.

'Tell me some more,' she said, wanting to know more about the obstacles, the desert and the sea. Wanting to know as much as possible to equip herself with knowledge to endure what lies ahead, in what was said to be one of the harshest environments on earth.

'Is the Sahara Desert in other parts of the world?' She asked ignorantly.

'No,' Victor responded.

'Although there are other deserts in the African continent and around the globe, however, the Sahara is the greatest in the world, occupying a huge part of Africa. It is like a bandana around the forehead of the continent, separating North Africa from Sub-Saharan Africa.

'The Sahara Desert has been a formidable obstacle to the aspiration of sub-Saharan African migrants like us, who intend to cross it to North Africa, which was only separated from Southern Europe by the Mediterranean Sea.

Judging by the hardship in Nigeria, I doubt if anyone would remain here, if not for that natural obstacle holding us.' Victor said with so much conviction, which made Mena to laugh.

She was not sure if it was the manner with which he said the words, or the stark reality of his statement, but she thought maybe she needed more of such laughs to ease the tension she felt.

'This was especially so in the 1990s,' Victor continued.

'That period, the number of Africans migrating to Europe was intensifying, although many African governments were in denial about the situation, or were downplaying the number of people leaving in droves. Yet, as the years went by many more African youths ventured abroad by any means, to seek greener pastures in the land of the white people.

'Although, a fraction of those who wanted to leave got legitimate visas to destinations in Europe and America, however, the vast majority of African migrants were not that fortunate. Again, while some were too poor to afford the expenses for the trip, others were affected by restrictive visa regimes by Western governments.

'That is why African migrants have worked out other means at attaining their goals, and many have made it to Europe using this method: through the Sahara Desert, and across the Mediterranean Sea to destinations in Spain, Italy etcetera,' Victor said.

He noticed Mena was now fast asleep, although he wanted to educate her some more. But he was happy he did not get to tell her the part that the desperation by African migrants to reach Europe, has become the deadliest form of human migration anywhere in the world. Hundreds of thousands of people have perished as a result of the dogged quest to take on the continental obstacles separating the two continents.

The daredevils mostly from West Africa, takeoff from communities at the fringes of the southern borders of the Sahara Desert, from whence they continue the macabre journey northwards to stations in North African.

If they succeeded, they would then be transported further north to coastal cities, especially in Libya and Morocco.

There they would join a boat to take them to Italy, Spain, or other European countries along the shores of the Mediterranean Sea.

Although there are several routes from North Africa to Europe via the Mediterranean Sea, however, Libya was the popular destination for the travelers. Consequently, many coastal cities in the country host millions of migrants, especially from Sub-Saharan countries, on a regular basis.

The four travelers arrived Jibia, in Jibia local government area of Kastina State, at the Northern fringes of the Nigerian border with Niger Republic around 2am. This was after a previous change of vehicle at Kano, a nearby state. There were no functional railway network transiting people between northern and southern Nigeria even as at 2015, so bus rides were mostly used for inter-state journeys across the motherland.

They were surprised by the cold which greeted them at that time of the night in the usually hot region, as they got off the bus. They had used the same transport company all through the journey from Benin City, in Southern Nigeria to Katsina.

All of them had their bags strapped across their shoulders as they made to inquire about the location of Niger Park, in Jibia.

Inside their bags was everything necessary for survival on the journey across the desert such as:

a water bottle, dry and durable foodstuff, a tooth brush, little tablets of soap, a short towel, a pair of sunglasses, a pair of T-shirts and a jacket. They were advised to travel light and to come with jackets, because of the dynamic weather conditions of the Sahara Desert.

Daba reached for his bag and took out his jacket for the cold was becoming unbearable. D1 did the same, while Mena clung to Victor as if her life depended on it.

'She's always going to be a drawback,' Daba thought as he walked past the couple to ask a fellow passenger who seemed like an indigene, about the direction to Niger Park.

There they hoped to board a vehicle for another two hours' drive to Kobo town, which has a long stretch of border with Niger Republic, Nigeria's northern neighbor.

'*Mena, to cross the Sahara Desert, no be beans o.*' Daba had said in vernacular, one evening as he sat with the couple at a bar. He was trying to describe the difficult terrain of the desert. Although he had said it jokingly, he was genuinely concerned about her safety in such a deadly environment. But he was careful how he expressed his worry about her participation in the journey, because he didn't want to seem like a spoiler. He however convinced himself that all would be well, especially as Jasmine was the one planning the mission and had promised to make the trip a little bearable.

But Mena did not see it that way. 'What a man can do, a woman can do as well, and sometimes even better.′ She would say to anyone with a discouraging comment about her joining the migrating group.

Victor shared Daba's concerns, though. He was in a dilemma. A part of him wanted to leave her behind, yet on the other hand he was willing to allow both of them take the risk. If they succeeded, they would have a lifetime of happiness together.

When the topic came up, he pretended to be super interested in what was happening in the African Champions League football match between ASEC Mimosas of Ivory Coast, and Eyimba FC of Aba, Nigeria, which was on display on a large screen at the far end of the bar. He prayed for a change of topic between his friend and his girlfriend, as Mena ranted on about her super woman capabilities.

Victor and Mena had intended to tie the knot, but for the dogged resistance against the union by Mena's parents. Mrs. Adekoko hated that Victor was jobless and was not the scion of a famous or wealthy parent, while for Mr. Adekoko it was his tribe.

'The Urhobos are too ambitious!' he is wont to say. What he really meant was, he did not like those Southern people from the Niger Delta region of the country.

The Adekoko's made their disapproval of the union between the lovebirds very clear, by arresting Victor on several occasions, as a point of discouraging them to be together.

The attempts to frustrate the relationship was proving to be effective, as Victor's departure date was drawing near.

So, Mena was forced to choose between taking the risk with him, or, to let Victor travel by himself, with no guarantee of returning to Nigeria, or to her.

The four of them trekked to Niger Park in less than ten minutes to meet a deserted place, with many vehicles parked in the dark.

'Men, this place is dark!' D1 exclaimed, when they got to the location. The Niger Park was the transit hub for people traveling to towns and villages located at the peripheries of the neighboring country. At the moment, a dim lamp in the middle of some food items and stationaries was the only source of light in the entire area. People enjoy abysmal electricity supply in many parts of rural Nigeria, thus the place was in darkness.

Luckily, MALLAM RABIU, the all-night shop keeper was graceful enough to provide them with two mats, which the journeymen placed their bags and rested to wait for day break.

As early as 5 am some drivers have begun to arrive at the park to do their car run; oil check and all, and to take turns in loading passengers. About an hour later the Nisan sedan they boarded was overloaded, with two people on the passenger's seat and four others at the back seat.

Some petty traders had also arrived and swarmed the vehicles loading passengers. They carried trays containing all sort of desert delicacies and herbs with the hope that the travelers might need something.

The driver who spoke in Hausa, urged the traders to give way as the journey was soon to begin. All the while the merchants continued to circle the car as they advertised their wares melodically in the lovely Hausa/Fulani dialect.

At Daba's request, a lady seated by his side explained the functions of some of the contents in the trays.

'This one is called *siffi,*' she began, pointing to something from one of the nearby trays filled with different stuff.

'It is good for desert fever, but it must not be taken before the sun comes up,' she instructed.

'This one here is *dokwa*,' the woman continued, taking a nut from one of the portions neatly arranged in the tray by a lanky boy, wearing the local *Aska Takwas* dress and a cap to match.

'*Nawa* (How much?)' She asked the boy in Huasa, and started cracking the nut with her teeth, before the hawker gave a reply.

'*Naira hamsin* (50 naira)' the boy responded with enthusiasm. His face shone as he anticipated the possibility of making his first sale that early in the morning.

'This fifty naira *dokwas* can sustain you for a whole day in the desert. But, you must not take more than one portion a day, else your stock of water for the whole journey won't be enough to quench your thirst, if you disobey the rule of the dokwas. If you maintain within a portion a day, there won't be any problem.

She pointed to other items in the tray and explained their functions to Daba and D1 who sat closest to her. Victor and Mena paid attention at the front seat, while the vendor stood throughout the explanation with one of his nuts already gone.

The travelers thanked the lady after the explanation, and collected some of the items like *siffi*, *dokwa* and another one known as *kongi*, which helps with hydration.

The ride through the arid Jibia land, which was sparsely dotted with short trees was interesting. They could see distances from any direction, as far as the eye could see, unlike the environment in southern Nigeria, littered with tall trees and bushes.

The trip across Nigeria came to a climax, as they arrived Kobo within two hours, as Jasmine had predicted.

After over twenty four hours on the road, it was at the border town of Kobo, that Daba and his friends finally had the opportunity to have their bath and refresh themselves.

They booked two rooms at a local hotel, where they are to wait till nighttime for the illegal crossing to Niger Republic.

It was easy for people in Kobo, and those from neighboring communities in Niger, to cross to either side, without much security checks.

For migrants, sometimes the "simple" crossing could not be that straightforward and an arrest by security operatives on the other side of the border, could be politicized by the government and lead to the premature termination of the journey for the affected migrant.

'We need to take our rest early to be in good shape for the motorcycle ride to Maradi, across the border this night,' Daba said. He and D1 had returned from making transportation arrangements for the next phase of the journey, and are now in Victor and Mena's hotel room to brief them. They came with takeaways including hot *akara* (Bean cake), fried plantain, yam, and soft drinks. They all stayed together after eating, until around noontime, before Daba and Victor left for the room which they shared.

After what seemed like just a few minutes, they heard repeated knocks on their door.

'Your bikes are here,' the hotel manager informed Daba, when he opened it. He looked at his watch and was surprised it was 8:15pm already.

'Thank you, Pantami,' Daba said and shut the door. He got his tooth brush and entered the small bathroom in the hotel room. D1 had had the first turn earlier in the day, so Daba went in first to have his bath, and asked D1 to inform the others that they were about to leave.

About twenty minutes later they mounted two motorcycles; Mena and Victor on one, while D1 and Daba took the other, as they steadied themselves for the next part of the journey to Maradi, a border town in Niger Republic.

Their ultimate destination was Germany, but they have to go through Niger, Libya and Italy as transit points. Jasmine had perfected plans to procure papers to get them to that country. Usually, an agent would collect $1, 800 to cover expenses for the whole trip from Nigeria to a location in Europe.

But they did not employ the services of an agent, instead Jasmine had provided a detailed step-by-step guide on how they will get to Libya, from whence he would take over their traveling plans.

They got to their first security stop after about 33km into Niger Republic.

There they met a small traffic and queued alongside others, while there was a similar queue on the opposite direction, with people on bikes, perhaps heading for Nigeria. Daba and his crew were easily let through after a $5 dollar bribe each.

They drove all night and encountered several check points, till they got to a location were hundreds of motorcycles were parked, to wait for day break.

By 6am, the set of motorcycles that brought Daba and his crew to the place had returned to Nigeria, while there were other bikes available for them to continue their journey to Maradi. The Nigerians negotiated a new ride, and by the first light of day, they were on their way.

As the day progressed the sun got brighter and hotter, making their keffiyehs to generate heat. But worst of all, was the amount of dust in the air and the hazy nature of the environment.

Sandstorms are common in the desert region and the people have learnt to live with it, but the same could not be said of the strangers on bikes who found the condition very irritating.

Daba thought the Nigeriens share a striking resemblance with his compatriots at the border towns of northwest Nigeria. They left him with a lasting impression, with their simplicity and display of contentment with life.

The villages they passed through on the long and tortuous voyage were the same. The people lived communally to survive under the harsh condition at the fringes of the Sahara Desert, and maximized the little agricultural opportunities therein.

As the day got brighter, the distance between the villages they passed through also became longer. They sometimes came across temporary settlements where they saw long distance merchants and their camels. They operated along the desert routes just as it was from time immemorial.

The heat became even more intense and brought to reality the difficulties which lay ahead of them on their quest for paradise. There was no turning back now.

For months, they've strategized on ways to breach the great Sahara obstacle, and the determination to do that was clear on each of their faces.

They sat quietly on the bikes with their shades on, as they squinted to prevent dust from getting into their noses.

Mena continuously wiped sweat off her pretty face, which had started to develop lines showing wariness.

They finally got to Maradi, the second largest city in Niger Republic, just before noontime, and the bikes dropped them off at a ghetto, as they were directed by Jasmine. There they stayed and waited for a vehicle that will take them to Agadez, the gateway to the Sahara Desert.

CHAPTER 7

THE MIEN

'The early mornings here are simply amazing, with the streets empty and the birds chirping under a stunning sunrise. One would think this is the most peaceful place on earth.' Jake said, using the statement and a handshake to welcome his guest who had arrived just on time.

'Don't get carried away by all that my friend,' KHALED JAMAL, the Libyan detective said after the handshake. He drew out a chair, and sat facing agent Jake in the open air café.

'The beauty of Libya can be infectious, strangers could get consumed by it,' Khaled said. He checked his watch to ensure he had attained his five-minutes-before-an-appointment principle, then settled himself on the cushion on the bamboo chair.

The tea shop operated by a Tunisian septuagenarian HAMDI MALEK, his wife and their two daughters was always open for business as early as 5am on daily basis, with the exception of Fridays. The open air service they offer used to be the delight of the elites in Tripoli, who occupy the seats, under the canopies, as soon as service was available. But with the crises in the country, the place was a shadow of itself. Only Jake and Khaled was at the place, out of fifty of such arrangements, as at 7am that morning.

'What do you have for me concerning the nocturnal organization?' Jake went straight to the point as soon as the busty NADIA, the younger of the two Hamdis left, after placing an order in front of the newly arrived guest.

Detective Khaled took a few sips from the thick, sweet tea in a small glass cup. He whipped the front of his T-shirt with both of his palms, although he did not spill a drink on it, then he began:

'You see,' he started.

'Before conflicts transcend into wars, many entities and individuals are usually involved in the direct, or remote causes and in sustaining of the hostilities.

'Their involvement could be either in the planning of the crisis, or through the supply of arms and ammunition to execute the war. That is where the Englishman John Mountbatten A.K.A. Mifta Rajab, comes into the scene.' Khaled stopped talking and went for another brief sipping session.

He continued, 'after things fell apart for the Redeemers following the death of their leader Hamuz Mohammed, in what is known here as "The Black Funeral," John Mountbatten struggled in hiding and was involved in different criminal activities to survive.

'However, by 2010 upwards, with the increasing militant activities in Libya, the Middle East, the African Chad Basin and parts of the Horn of Africa, Mifta Rajab had become a key player in arms trading in the region. He also provided services, including human cargo and drugs transportation within his domain.

'These days however,' Khaled went on. 'He uses a shipping line called La Voyage to transport cargoes. Our sources say the goods are tied to a chain underneath the ship to avert detection by the authorities, thereby enabling him to bring illegal materials to the shores of North African Mediterranean coastlines without being detected.

'The cargos upon arrival in North Africa, are thence transported by a unit of the Clique known as the MIEN, which carry out logistics operations for the organization either within Libya, or to and fro locations across Mifta Rajab's territory.

'This unit is also sort of like the military arm of the nefarious institution, which implements missions on behalf of the body. Their activities usually transcends anything that has to do with the physical execution of the objectives of the Clique.'

'What does the acronym M-I-E-N mean?' Jake interrupted.

'The name is not an abbreviation,' Detective Khaled answered.

'I believe it was derived from the way we Libyans pronounce the English word "MEN,"' Khaled clarified. However, the group is composed of smart young boys and girls who take care of issues for the organization as a team, no matter how important or trivial the assignment may be.

'The unit is comprised of WILSON, a migrant from Uganda. He was also known as CPU, because of his expertise with computers, and his vast information communication technology skills. His job is to feed the team with intelligence on basically everything they needed to know about a specific mission, after it had been assigned to the MIEN by the Clique.

'Other members of the MIEN include two sisters from Somalia AISHA and AMINA, and their brother HAGGI. They had fled their homeland after their father, a tribal leader from the semi-autonomous state of Puntland, was brutally murdered alongside two of their siblings by government forces in their town of Bosaso. They had managed to escape to Libya where Haggi become a port rat and his sisters, Amina and Aisha port girls.'

'What is the connection between the girls and the Clique?' Jake who had been listening carefully, asked for clarity.

The question gave Khaled another opportunity to reach for the small cup of tea, then he readied himself again, before responding to the question.

'You see, the Somalians and Jasmine, the coordinator of the MIEN go way back. They used to hang around the Port de Tripoli, where they did menial jobs to survive, either as loaders working for agents offloading cargos, or getting involved in any sharp practice to make ends meet.

'Moreover, other members of the MIEN are four Libyan youths ABDO FARAJ, AZIZ SALAM, MUSTAFA HAMZA and MARWAN MAHMUD. They are the local component of the group, including an Algerian OMAR HAKIM. They have been a vital source of local intelligence and direction, both in Libya and in the region,' Khaled said.

'Two additional ad hoc MIEN may be recruited and placed on standby for every mission and could be called upon as circumstance may demand. They could be sent to replace one of the MIEN in an active field, or they could be factored in an imminent operation.

'Like I said earlier,' Khaled kept on. 'Jasmine A.K.A. *Jamin*, is the coordinator of the MIEN, and coincidentally was himself the first recruit of this very important unit of the Clique's operation mechanism.

'Initially, the unit was incorporated into the organization as a body responsible for the transportation of human cargos, migrants, drugs and other illegal stuff. Lately however, they have become more involved in arms transportation from their base in Libya, to countries at the fringes of the lower end of the Sahara Desert, parts of Central Africa and in East Africa.

'Their first major operation for the Clique was at Sirt, where their mission was to intercept a truck heading to Tripoli from Benghazi, with a mandate to retrieve the merchandise it carried. The goods inside the vehicle had been seized by the authorities there. The lorry had been identified to contain suspicious contents and was being taken to the headquarters in Tripoli for further investigation, when the MIEN struck.

'Here are some pictures from the attack,' he reached for an envelope inside his jacket and handed it to the INTERRPOL agent.

'The MIEN must have been furnished with all the necessary data regarding the logistics arrangement of the truck and the security details. We suspect the involvement of Wilson, the Ugandan computer whiz kid, who must have provided much of the technical support, including information on the best location for the attack and perhaps, the number of security personnel assigned to protect the cargo.

'Wanted in his country for a hacking escapade gone wrong, he now deploys his skills excellently for the MIEN.' Khaled said.

The ambidextrous INTERPOL agent took points at intervals on a note which fits into the palm of his right hand. It was like he was taking lecture points, as the Libyan detective reeled out the information about the MIEN.

The Libyan official knowing he had the attention of the American, kept on ditching out the information he had been contracted to deliver out of the official channel.

'The MIEN had set up an ambush for the truck at Sirte, about 450km from Tripoli,' he continued.

'There the Algerian, the four Libyans and two ad hoc MIEN pretended their van had developed a fault, as they waited for the convoy that was heading to Tripoli. The Somali sisters were spotted in front of the truck and am sure their brother Haggi, must have been with Jasmine, somewhere in the background.

'They opened fire on the convoy after they had put it in disarray with several explosions, 200 meters from the attack point. The security personnel who had survived the commotion scampered for their lives, while a gallant few returned fire.

'The team succeeded that day, but not without a setback, as one of the pioneer members of the unit Marwan Mahmud, lost his life in that operation.

'Haggi, who had appeared from nowhere during the transfer of the cargo to their truck was also shot in the leg, before they fled the scene.

'They had quickly transferred the goods which were in crates into their truck and drove off, leaving some parts of the road messed up by the explosions.

'Inside those crates were dozens of AK47 automatic rifles, fifty Rocket Propelled Grenades (RPG's), and hundreds of live ammunition.

'I must add,' Khaled said, as a way of rounding off.

'Following that operation at Sirte, Jasmine became the Englishman's Man Friday, and effectively oversaw the arms deals in the desert area. He was in charge of handling the desert guards and other security agencies, to ensure the smooth transportation of cargoes down south.

'Again, just like his boss before him, Jasmine had rapidly rose in influence. He has created a niche for himself along the timeless Trans-Sahara trade routes, where a good percentage of illegal materials are still being transported in, and out of sub-Sahara Africa.

'Also like john Mountbatten, Jasmine's rising influence in the Clique has somewhat exposed him to enemies big and small, thus making him a high target in Libya.

'I must be on my way,' Detective Khaled said, and made to take his leave, leaving the documents on the attack at Sirte with Agent Jake.

'You must know by now that the Clique has transcended into bigger things, as opposed to the illegal migration activities you have focused you investigations on.' Khaled said.

'You might as well arrest the people you see on the streets, because everyone in Tripoli seems to be involved in the business of migrating people to Europe, one way or the other.

'I have so much on my plate at the office this morning, he said after a solid handshake with the INTERPOL agent, and took his leave.

Jake was left with the thought that Mifta Rajab was indeed a big fish in the criminal underworld in Libya and the entire region, but he was discouraged that the man was not the person INTERPOL needed at the moment. The worsening migration situation around the Mediterranean Sea was their initial purpose of coming after organizations like the Clique, and individuals like Mifta Rajab. He decided to lay more emphasis on finding Jasmine, as he may end up being a vital piece in the investigation.

CHAPTER 8

THE DESERT GUARDS

'The Sahara Desert is an unending sand sea. If you pee in it, it dries out within seconds.' LUKEMAN, a co-traveler and compatriot, told the Nigerians at the ghetto in Maradi.

They have been at the place for five days now, waiting for the vehicle that will take them to Agadez. Lukeman on the other hand, was in his third week at the shanty town. He seemed to know everything about the journey and he was also a good storyteller.

'My townsperson who had crossed the Sahara Desert on this same journey said, during their journey to Agadez, they were arranged at the back of a lorry like they were in a canoe, one migrant lapping another, with watermelon and leaves placed on top of their heads for cover from the authorities.' Lukeman said.

When Lukeman spoke he seemed to look towards the direction of Mena, perhaps due to the obvious fright on her face inspired by his stories. Victor for an unknown reason was taking notes from what Lukeman was saying, while D1 and Daba also paid attention.

Day and night, the dirty heap at the back edge of the slum was a favorite meeting point for the migrants, as they waited for the departure to the Gateway to the Sahara Desert. All kinds of drugs were freely sold and used at the spot, while prostitution and gambling were also commonplace.

Lukeman had developed the habit of seeking the four friends out at the ghetto, where they were always seen together. He would praise Mena to the high heavens for her elegance and beauty, before proceeding to beg her for some money to buy something to smoke.

His stories mostly began when the smoke was halfway, and he was a chain smoker.

'My friend said they passed through at least seven check points on their way, where officers would use pointed sticks to poke into spaces in the heap of water melon, if they suspected that migrants could be hiding inside the carriage of the truck.

'He said "anyone who got pierced dared not scream, else they were all doomed."'

At this point Lukeman had finished rolling and spitting a new stick of smoke, which he stretched to D1, to take the first drag. He watched him keenly, as he took a few puffs from it, and then passed it on to Daba.

Lukeman faced Mena again, and continued his story. 'Unfortunately, my friend got duped by an agent in Tripoli, and he ended up staying in Libya for five years, where he worked hard to survive like he never did in Nigeria.

'He made me to understand that we Nigerians work very hard abroad, but we are hindered by ego and a bad system, to do same in the motherland.

'He remained in Libya and was optimistic he could gather enough money for the crossover to Europe. He was eventually arrested and deported, alongside hundreds of illegal migrants in a major raid that year.

'The guy stayed in Lagos for many years after the deportation, due to the shame of returning to our hometown empty-handed. Plus, he had done some bad stuff before leaving Kogi state, where we came from. He had even sold a vital family land to make up for the failed trip to Europe.

'However, he summoned the courage and returned home. His father forgave him, and even married a wife for him to settle down.

'Today, he is a sprawling businessman in Kogi, with his own house and a lovely family.' Lukeman said, dropped the smoke and smashed the butt with his hardened Timberland boots.

That was the last time they saw him, because immediately after his interesting story, a callout began across the ghetto:

"VICTOR!"

"DABA!"

"D1!"

"MENA!"

Two men shouted from different directions at the slum. Their vehicle had arrived, and all was ready for the next phase of their journey to Agadez.

Maradi to Agadez was just about half a day's drive, but migrant's agents could keep their clients in camps for weeks awaiting the journey, due to what they termed "security reasons". Yet, they collected taxes for each day the migrants spent at the safe houses.

After over ten hours' drive in arid condition, they arrived Agadez, where Daba, Victor, Mena and D1 were taken to a migrants' haven known as *Dar*.

Dar was under the protection of armed militia group who collected taxes to provide security for the illegal operation. Jasmine had also informed them on how they would get to the location when they arrived

The safe house was a popular transit point for African migrants heading to towns close to the Libyan border with Niger Republic.

Similar to the strategy at Maradi, migrant's agents could keep their clients at Dar for up to ten days, to organize the trip to their next destination. But that was not the case with the crew from southern Nigeria.

TCHIMA SARATOU, the coordinator of operations at Dar, had given Daba and the others special preference at the safe house in Agadez, after they identified themselves as acquaintances of Jasmine, upon their arrival at the place. He was the one who also personally handled the arrangements for a vehicle that would take them to Al-Qatron, a border town in Southern Libya, where they would link up with Gyadhi.

He even provided four small mattresses in a private room for the crew throughout their stay in Dar. This was indeed, a rare luxury at the migrants' center, where up to fifty people could be kept in one place at a time.

Tchima had also provided the Hilux van for the journey and reserved the passenger's and the back seats for the four Nigerian travelers. Twenty other migrants occupied the outer part of the van.

The males among them sat at the edge of the truck, with their legs hanging out, while holding a stick for support.

The driver had carried additional kegs of petrol for refill in the desert and two spare tires. He drove at full speed and made occasional stops at some trading centers and villages, where the passengers were allowed some time to buy food and water or other items for refreshment. They usually spent the nights at old roadhouses. Some of these desert haven have existed since ancient times and they afforded travelers the platforms to take the necessary rest after a tiring course.

The four days drive to Al Qatron was agonizing. The four of them had difficulties in breathing caused by the dusty roads and sweltering heat. Yet, at nighttime the desert environment could be unbearably cold.

Although they have set their minds on these eventualities, however the reality was somewhat a different ball game. Especially as time seems to go a little bit slower under such tough conditions, thereby psychologically extending the duration of the grueling journey.

After a seemingly unending expedition across the desert, they finally stopped at a desert village for a rest. There the company was divided into two groups which were allocated to separate huts as accommodation for the night.

Daba couldn't sleep all through the night. He left the hut to sit among a small cycle of men doing puff-puff-pass with a hookah. They sat surrounding a fire and spoke rapidly in Arabic. He found a space among them close to where the driver of their truck sat and joined in. They continued their conversation and ignored him, but he was glad to get his share of the smoke when it came around. His lack of proper sleep for consecutive days had resulted in constant migraines, but his condition was a small matter compared to that of the only female member of the crew.

Mena had taken ill the night before they left Agadez, and she has been very weak all through the day's journey. Her situation had made the travelers to make a few stops in the middle of nowhere, due to concerns over her breathing difficulties.

The next day however, she was feeling better as they returned to the Hilux van before sunrise. As usual, the driver did a head count of passengers on board the vehicle, and they resumed their journey as early as 5.30 am.

Daba felt a sense of relief each time they were on the move.

It gave him a reason to believe that they were getting closer to their scheduled meeting place with Gyadhi, and their overall destination.

After an hour into their journey, suddenly their almost seamless drive took a negative turn. Now, they were faced with one of the most dreaded law enforcement agencies in the world, known as the Nigerien Desert Guards, NDG.

Disasters of certain shapes and magnitude could take only a few seconds to manifest, and such was the situation which the migrants found themselves at that moment. Some of the men at the back of the Hilux instinctively took flight heading towards a valley beside the hilly road, despite the orders not to move by the rifle-wielding security personnel.

Among the escapees was D1, who continued his desperate run, driven by the heat of the moment. He was oblivious of shouts from his friends for him to stop. He fell, rolled over on the hot sand, stood up and continued on his desperate attempt to nowhere.

Definone had that day, left his position in-between Daba and Victor at the back seat, to join those sticking out their legs at the edge of the lorry. He had complained bitterly about the heat inside the van which he found unbearable. Following their escape, the desert guards rounded off the remaining occupants of the lorry and relocated them to one of the two vans they had arrived with.

Interestingly Victor, Mena and Daba were allowed to remain in their positions inside the Hilux van, while the other migrants were transferred to one of the NDG vehicles, as they were being transferred to Bilma, where the regional station of the Desert Guards was situated up north. One of the NDG vans rode in front, and the other at the rear, while the vehicle conveying Daba and the crew was in the middle.

After a comprehensive profiling at Bilma, the arrested migrants will be transferred to Niemay, the administrative headquarters of Niger Republic, from whence they will be deported to their countries of origin.

The Nigerien Desert Guard, formerly the Division Daguet, was initially established by the

French, during colonial era, and oversaw a good portion of territories on the western part of the Sahara desert.

The primary function of the Division Daguet, was to ensure security along the French territories within the Sahara Desert. They also embark on rescue missions when the situation arises.

The NDG as the division was known today, only came about after Niger Republic attained her independence in August, 1960.

Moreover, due to the steady rise in number of migrant casualties in the desert, especially from the 1980s and 1990s, most governments in the countries bordering the Sahara Desert, took steps to upgrade their border protection networks. This led to the implementation of strict policies to deter the easy illegal migration of people in and out of their borders.

Niger Republic located at the northern parts of West Africa, occupied a good portion of the southern end of the Sahara Desert. She is one of the key migration concerned nations which had also implemented policies to improve its border security system.

This was especially so following the 1995 discoveries of twenty-one corpse, and twenty three decomposing bodies at separate locations in Bilma, suspected to be leftovers of migrants from Sub-Saharan Africa, who might have been abandoned by their transporters.

Today, more desert guards have been employed to man the borders. In addition to the provision of more patrol vehicles for logistic support and to aid the conduct of reconnaissance missions. These measures had proved to be effective in deterring many prospective migrants from embarking on the deadly journey across the Sahara in the early periods of the implementation of the policies.

However, the overwhelming number of people who still took the risk to get to Europe on foot through Niger, far outnumbered the number of the NDG personnel by over a hundred to one. Coupled with the infiltration of corrupt elements into the system. Thus, illegal migration operation networks like the Clique, continued to wield great influence in the area, despite the improving number of security presence in the desert.

Some top-ranking officers of NDG were on the payroll of the Clique, and does the bidding of Mifta Rajab and his cohorts.

Including the ones who are currently aiding the passage of three special Nigerian migrants, on their way to Al-Qatron.

In the meantime, the concern of the NDG officials who had just arrested the migrants using the Hilux, was how to explain the whereabouts of the missing Nigerian to Jasmine. Although they have conceded that the situation would no doubt, affect their final payment for the deal.

Meanwhile, for the remaining three members of the crew, the whole ordeal had completely dashed their hopes of making it to Libya. Daba and Victor sat quietly in the truck and wondered how they would be able to start all over again, if they were deported back to Nigeria.

Mena had fallen ill again and she rested her head by the wound down glass of the door at the passenger's seat of the truck, under the scotching sun. Her health had continued to deteriorate as the hours went by. Victor could not be of much help as he was at the back seat of the van.

Suddenly, the truck in front of the convoy began to slow down, while the other at the rear sped off, with the other captured emigrants on board. After the first car came to a halt, two officers came out with bags like those from a fast-food joint. They got to the other car which had also stopped and gave a package to each of the captured migrants inside, and their driver. And just like that the nightmare took a pleasant turn.

The travelers were allowed to take a peek into the bag to find out that the content had indeed come from a nice restaurant. Soon the car was filled with the aroma of roasted beef and other nice looking stuff.

'This must be a miracle,' Daba said to himself, as he removed his gaze from the bag and looked at the desert guard who had presented it to him. He thought something must be fishy.

'Eat.'

One of the guards with an aura of superiority amongst them spat out, with a native accent.

Other items in the package include a freshly baked bread, slices of fresh tomatoes, vegetables and a not-so-too-long-ago roasted chicken. Each pack also came with a liter of fresh milk, and water.

The crew could not contain their delight over the turn of events. Mena in her naughty fashion jumped on a tall black guard, who maintained his posture as she kissed him on both chicks. While the others took turns to shake hands with the guards with unreserved joy.

The one who seemed to be the leader, explained how Jasmine had arranged for their safe passage across the heavily fortified area, leading to the border between Niger and Libya. They assured the three of them that they would be delivered safely to Gyadhi in Al-Qatron.

The incident did not only bring relief to the emigrants, but also strengthened their belief that the mission to Europe will be successful.

The NDG officials took their leave after a little argument with SANI, the driver. They blamed him for the disappearance of D1. He had been instructed to keep Jasmine's immigrants inside his truck. They faulted his decision to allow D1 relocate to the back of the van in the first place.

The personnel were still visibly angry about the missing man as they got into their vehicle and zoomed off, leaving the travelers to go at their own pace.

From then on, the journey went in the manner it was before their arrest by the NDG officials. The van this time was speedier as it had been relieved of its load, after the other migrants were taken away by the NDG. They continued with the same routine of making a few stops for shelter and food, and being on the road thirteen hours each day.

They were only held up for a few minutes at the Nigerien border with Libya, where Sani paid $50 for each of his passengers and they were let through without further troubles.

They finally arrived at al-Qatron in the morning of the fourth day of the journey to the delight of all the travelers.

Sani the driver cum desert guide, who had received instructions on Gyahdi's location at the border town, took them straight to meet him.

The Nigerians met Gyadhi at a large compound, sitting on a mat under a black tent. Two of his assistants MUSA and ABU, were there doing his bidding.

Aside being an indigene of the place, the house at Al-Qatron was symbolic for Gyadhi's work along the desert routes, while his wife and nine children reside in his other house in Tripoli.

The journey had been tedious for Mena, Daba and Victor. They fell on one another on the large mat under the tent upon getting to where Gyadhi was, without the courtesy to greet their host first.

Gyadhi had been informed about what happened to D1 in the desert, but he was still anxious to hear from the crew members what really transpired out there.

'Where is the fourth person?' He asked, looking at the Nigerians for a while, and then to the driver who brought them.

Sani, who was tired of answering questions about D1's whereabouts, quickly gave the excuse that he was in a hurry to meet up with his superiors at their base in al-Qatron, and left horridly.

Gyadhi bid him farewell, returned his gaze to his guests and asked: 'Who among you is Daba?'

'Daba responded by lifting the chilled bottle of water presented to him by Musa, who had brought light refreshments for the travelers, and sat up to answer what seemed like imminent questions from Gyadhi.

'You are supposed to be four, what happened?' Gyadhi asked again. This time directing the question to him.

Daba went on to tell him about the arrival of the desert guards and their sporadic shooting, which frightened the emigrants in the Hilux, especially those who were exposed to gunfire at the back of the truck. And how D1 escaped into the valley.

Gyadhi scratched his head, after paying steadied attention to Daba's explanation, and thought it tallied with what the desert guards had said, when they called to inform him about the incident. But the Libyan driver remained unsatisfied. He detested failure in job execution especially, an incomplete job. He does not take excuses from his subordinates and now he was about to deliver three persons to Jamin, when he was expecting four.

'Don't worry,' he assured his guest.

'They say Jamin has been informed about the situation, and he had given the orders that D1 be rescued at any cost.' He said.

It was later in the evening that the thought of D1 and concerns about his safety really began to dawn on his friends. They have regained some strength as the day wears out. Nighttime had also brought relief from the effect of the scorching sun they had been under all day.

Gyadhi turned out to be a very good host. He instructed his stewards to take care very good care of his guests. They all ended up spending the night around a thick fireplace, where the very entertaining Gyadhi talked all evening, and told them the story of Africa and Eura.

CHAPTER 9

AFRICA AND EURA

'The fate of the people of Africa and that of the continent of Europe are intertwined, one cannot be separated from the other.' Gyadhi began, as he got set to tell his favorite story to the Nigerian migrants.

He spurned from his mat and rested on his right elbow, in that, he was now positioned facing the migrants from West Africa, as he told them the story of Africa and Eura.

Gyadhi always shared the story whenever he came across Africans immigrating to Europe. He called it his "humanitarian effort" towards ending the scourge of migration in Africa. It was motivated by his firsthand knowledge of the life consuming situation in the Sahara Desert, where thousands of youths from West, East and Central Africa have perished attempting to cross it, on their way to the fringes of the Mediterranean Sea in North Africa, with Europe in focus.

'Africa was once paradise.' Gyadhi started.

'A place where everything good and pleasant can be found, and the people were healthy, joyful and very peaceful.

'Because the people lived in paradise, they developed a communal way of life where there was no competition for anything, as everything they needed was available for them in surplus.

'According to the story, Africa has three sisters: Eura, Antica and Asia; and two brothers, Strialia and America.

'One day their father King Earth, called for a feast of many colors to commemorate his uncountable years on the throne.

'"Prepare for a great banquet!"' He thundered with excitement, as he informed his children about the special occasion.

'"I will share an important information at the opening event of the festivities,"' He also announced.

'On the fateful day, the King reclined on his big white chair with a large table of colors separating him from his children. All of them too were adorned in their favorite colors, as they sat before him.

'The King had a steady grin on his face, as he thought of how quickly the children have come of age. He was convinced that the time has come to divide his vast kingdom among them, and himself into them including his splendor, might and shortcomings.

'He went on to reveal his intention to split them into his various estates across the globe. He advised them to be competitive and ensure to preserve, and survive in each of the regions which they would find themselves.

'Then the King got up from his chair and showed them a vision from a frame on his huge throne. It was like a massive Sony TV, fashioned to a white space behind the royal seat.

'From it they could see the different shades of the continents before them. Some white and beautiful, others green and lovely, while there were yellow and vast ones too. There were also those surrounded by a great body of water, and another where the sun resides.

'King Earth turned his attention from the screen and faced Africa, his eldest child. '"I wept the day you were born," he said, maintaining his gaze on her, as he crossed over to the table where the children were seated and clasped his palms on Africa's cheeks.

'"So beautiful and radiant, I held you in my arms that day, and prayed for more of you to come. Indeed, I have been blessed with so many lovely children after you,"' the King said. He spoke directly to her, thus sweeping the large hall with a strong wave of emotion, due to the manner in which Earth addressed his firstborn.

'Inwardly, the king was agitated, because he had serious concerns over the welfare of his beloved Africa, if he left them to fend for themselves. But what has to be done has to be done, he knew.

'He was genuinely worried because of her penchant for charity and gullibility, two attributes he feared would not hold water in the competitive world that will soon follow.

'He kept a hand on Africa's cheek and used the other hand to beckon on the other children to gather for a big hug, almost squatting so he could reach all of them.

'After a moment in a warm embrace the King rose and returned to his throne. He turned to Africa again and said:

'"As my first child, you shall have the privilege to choose first from one of the continents which I shall present before you, and your brothers and sisters today.

'"But first, you must take a color,"' King Earth said, and stepped aside to watch as they made their choices.

'Having prior knowledge of their divergent fortunes, he cautioned the children to be wise in making their decisions, as their fate will be bound to the choices they made. He emphasized that each of them must preserve whatever portion of the earth they found themselves.

'King Earth however assured them that they will survive in the different regions because, even his weaknesses have been a source of strength in his very long years of existence.

'Africa then went before the large table of colors and took one, and the others followed suit, until each of them had taken a color. All of them retaining their favorite colors.

'While Africa took a portion of the earth which was rosy and endowed with virtually all the natural minerals in the world with a vast area of arable land, the case was not the same for some of her siblings.

'Some chose the portion of the globe that was riddled with conflicts, others took the section of the earth with too much sun. A few of them picked the area with too much water, or snow. Yet still, some got the part with environmental challenges like earthquakes, volcanos and tornados.

'Nevertheless, the people of Africa lived in peace and harmony in their communal ways.' Gyadhi said, and paused, to weigh the attention level of his audience, before he continued.

'Things were truly promising for Africa at that time, until the sudden reunion with one of her sisters Eura, after millions of years apart.' Gyadhi stopped talking again, and took two long drags from a pipe attached to a *shisha* pot presented to him by Abu. He took two more drags and returned the object to the apprentice, who received it and knelt by his side dutifully.

The Libyan continued:

'It all began when Eura, through the activities of prospectors and seafarers from her domain, took adventures to the waters of the world, in the last age of discovery and conquest. She had previously come in contact with Asia, her immediate elder sister and America, the last born of the family. She was truly on a quest to conquer the world.

To her advantage, she noticed upon reestablishing contact with her eldest sister, that African is still as she was, when earth was one big paradise.

'Everything was still beautiful and in abundance, and the people shared natures many gifts in a communal bliss.

'Alas, Africa's simplistic and communal-centric culture was no match for the capitalist Eura, whose hostile environment and conflict ridden continent, has necessitated a stronger survival instinct and a penchant for industry. These factors have motivated her to achieve the earliest feat of conquering earth's most formidable continental dividers, including the seas and oceans of the world.

'Armed with the knowledge which she had acquired over the centuries, she went on to cross the Atlantic Ocean; one of the greatest continental obstacles separating Africa and Eura.

'On that historic day, Eura came crying:

'"Africa, my dearest Africa, I have missed you!"'

'She sobbed uncontrollably as she ran through the long passage leading to the throne where Africa was seated.

'Africa too, on seeing her long lost little sister, jumped from her throne and ran to meet Eura, for she was indeed happy to see her again.

'She organized a great feast to welcome her sister and gathered all her healthiest youth; the strongest African men and the most beautiful African maidens and presented them before their long lost aunty Eura. She gave Eura a family time of her life. Africa did not realize that Eura had an ulterior motive to conquer and colonize her continent.

'The long and short of the story is that, Eura achieved her objective of obtaining vital resources from Africa to develop her own continent and ruled the world.'

Gyadhi did not stop. He continued.

'Eura went on to use her military might, and a powerful religion she acquired from the Middle East, to lure and subjugate Africa into giving out her choicest youths and natural resources.

'The Atlantic Ocean could not hold back the tears as she watched the injustice by one sibling on another in the name of survival. Many ships conveying Africans as slaves to Eura drowned at sea, because of the droplets coming from her eyes.

'Hundreds of thousands of quality Africans, men and women perished in the Atlantic Ocean, whilst being transported to Euraland. Their spirits are haunting the two continents to this day. They are still attracting the youths in Africa to Europe from all angles: by air, through the Mediterranean Sea, and even across the Sahara Desert.

'Africa is still being punished for her inability to be competitive and for letting Eura have her resources, whether by brute or guile.

'The curse holds till this day, and you guys are a manifestation to this truth.'

Gyadhi concluded as he pointed his index finger to the migrants who were spread across the mat. Only Victor and Daba were still awake to listen to the concluding part of the story. By now Mena was fast asleep.

'Moreover,' Gyadhi started again, as if he wanted to tell the story afresh.

'You should know that even Eura did not have her cake and eat it. Because, she was herself swindled by their little brother America, whom she had channeled most of her energy and resources towards developing.

'But the feat she attained in surmounting the seas and oceans, which were the greatest natural obstacles to the movement of people between continents, made Eura to rule over the earth for a long time. Her network of territories was later transformed into something like a global marketplace. Unfortunately, Africa still remains at the lowest rung of the trading arrangement.'

After saying that, Gyadhi took one last drag from the third pot of shisha that had been lit for him that evening. Then he stretched his large frame on the mat and said, 'good night my people.'

'Good night' Victor responded. He was particularly stunned by the astonishing tale told by the Libyan. He felt the story of Africa and Eura perfectly reflected the origins of Africa's predicament.

Victor took another look at Gyadhi, who within seconds was already snoring, and then turned to check Mena's temperature, by placing the back of his hand to her neck.

'Maybe there is more to the freestyle demeanor Gyadhi was portraying,' he suspected, as he put his arm across Mena's body to sleep.

Musa and Abu rounded off their Stewards-of-The-Year performance by interchanging watch, as the company had their night rest under the canopy in the open field.

CHAPTER 10

THE CONTACT PERSON

By 2015, the number of people from Africa and the Middle East who were willing to risk their lives to get to Europe, had reached a crescendo. Its effect was felt mostly in Libya, which by this time played host to hundreds of thousands of migrants annually.

The corresponding magnitude of deaths from boat accidents in the attempt to bridge the continental divide, also took a terrifying dimension in the years following the Syrian Civil War in 2015, leading to the displacement of many people from that country.

While millions of Syrians sought refuge in neighboring countries like Turkey and Lebanon, others in droves made the daring attempt to reach Europe by crossing the Mediterranean Sea, thus escalating the already vibrant migration activities in North Africa.

The situation offered migrant's agents in Libya, and their collaborators in Italy and Spain, the opportunity to channel some of their clients to locations in German and Sweden. And other countries in Europe, who have opened their gates to the Syrian migrants at the height of the European migration crisis, by the middle of that year.

Many in Sub-Saharan Africa also spotted the opportunity presented by the development. This also increased the number of migrants especially from West Africa, attempting to reach North Africa through the Sahara Desert, and then to Europe, via the Mediterranean Sea.

The Syrian crisis thus became the latest avenue for migrants to take advantage of national tragedies elsewhere, by pretending to be victims from such countries, in order to seek asylum to Europe and America. The situation also increased the number of casualties at both the Saharan and Mediterranean obstacles.

Jasmine reflected on these things and felt a deep pain for what has become of his people, and wished he could do something about it.

The wars, coups and countercoups, and corruption have affected the growth of the black section of the continent, despite attempts by the impoverished people to rise above their problems.

Even the seeds of democracy planted in many African countries, was yet to develop firm roots and was usually no match for the monstrous form of African nepotism and corruption, which has contributed to crippling the continent as she endures her curse.

"Another 116 African Migrants Drown off Mauritanian Coast" - was the bold headline on the National Light, a popular Libyan daily, which he was reading absentmindedly.

The caption reminded Jasmine of Gyadhi's famous story of Africa and Eura, as he dropped the paper on the table, and went to the window, of the now smaller hotel room which he had relocated to for the night, and did another round of lookout.

Jasmine had put the TV off in compliance with Omon's "zero-noise order," to allow her to have some sleep. He took a look at her, as she dozed off, but he could not do the same.

The latest incident in the news had occurred when a small boat cramped with over a hundred migrants had drowned in the Atlantic Ocean, off the Mauritanian coastline. They had attempted to reach Morocco, whose shortest distance to Spain in Europe, was a little over a dozen kilometers across the Mediterranean Sea. There were no survivors.

Using the Mauritanian waters to get to the Morocco, and then to its Mediterranean coastline, was a favorite shortcut taken by many African migrants who intend to partially avoid the Sahara Desert route. However, this pathway has had its fair share of migrants' casualties over the decades.

'How has it come to this?' Jasmine wondered.

'People everywhere have found a way to cope with their environments and prospered, be it in the Arctic North, or under the scorching sun in the Middle East. So, what is holding Africa?' he pondered some more.

Jasmine felt genuine concern for the black race, and worried if there was any hope for the continent, if she continues to shed her blooming flowers.

He remembered how incredibly brilliant Victor was back home, and how he seemed to know almost everything from the sciences to the arts.

'If only Africa has got a working formula for her youths, someone like Victor would have been an excellent patriot for his country, instead of risking his life in the desert to come here,' Jasmine reflected. With that thought, he got off from worrying for his country and continent, to focus on the issues at hand. There was palpable danger in Libya, and he had to make some pragmatic decisions.

Their relocation to the new hotel in southern Tripoli was one of the precautionary measures he had taken so far. This was not just to address the imminent danger, but it was a cautionary move, as rumors of complete collapse of the oil rich nation by warring factions gather momentum.

These factors, coupled with recent happenings in Jasmine's life, such as the incident with the two guys at the bank, and the meeting with Kharig in the next few hours, contributed to heighten the paranoia he has been feeling of late.

He had received message from Gyadhi that the crew have been delivered to him safely, with the exception of D1, which he had issued directives for his recue.

The rest of the crew are expected to arrive in Tripoli within the next few days, so arrangements must be made for the next and final stage of their journey, which is the crossover.

Jasmine understood perfectly what his friends must have gone through by now. The hunger, the thirst, the hostile winds and the fuming sun, and he was determine to give them a treat irrespective of the tension in town; and to ensure their smooth transition to Europe.

He still remembered like it was yesterday, when he left his mother's warm embrace that early morning in July, before heading into the world with Europe in sight.

He reflected on his experience in the Sahara Desert, which was by all means cruder than what his friends were going through currently, because he had no one to help him during his time.

Plus, he had a travel arrangement where they had to trek long distances in Niger Republic on foot, to make up part of the journey.

Also, most of the vehicles for transporting people across the Sahara as at that time were rickety and unfit for a long journey. Sometimes the travelers could remain at a spot for days, due to a broken down vehicle.

His agent AHMED, had abandoned him at Agadez, where he had ran out of funds in the middle of the journey. He had underestimated the cost for the mission then, in addition to other unforeseen circumstances he met after leaving the borders of Nigeria.

He would have died of hunger and disease at the safe house in Agedez, if not for Gyadhi who took him into his company. He had said he liked what he called "the young man's determination." Before the encounter with the Libyan transporter, Jasmine had been at the congested place for over eight weeks.

Gyadhi then took Jasmine to a popular Cameroonian agent named AUDU, at Sabha, in Libya, before returning to the desert for his next pick up.

The months of July and August were said to be the peak of the migration season, when the Mediterranean Sea was calmer. But the same could not be said of the Sahara Desert within the same time frame, where temperatures could reach as high as 40 degrees Celsius. Strangely, it was also a period for long distance drivers like Gyadhi to make the big bucks.

Gyadhi and Audu had agreed that Jasmine would work under him to gather enough money for his journey to Tripoli and across the sea to Italy.

In little over six months, Jasmine was able to work his way to Tripoli, after settling all agreements with Audu. But he again ran out of luck when in his first night in Tripoli, the authorities raided the cheap hotel he had put up, in search of illegal migrants.

He escaped, but lost all of his savings he had kept in his bag, which he left at the place. Thus, yet again, he was unable to come up with the money for the crossover to Italy.

That was how he became a wharf rat for over a month in Tripoli, after the remaining $40 he was left with had been exhausted. Until the fortunate encounter with John Mountbatten, his boss.

So he has been there, done that. He has a good understanding of what a man would need after a trip across the Sahara Desert.

Jasmine stood by the window, in the middle of the night at 1a.m, to make some calls. He made arrangements for a private dinner with Omon the following day. He also made series of calls after that: one to a member of the Clique, and another to a senior officer in the Libyan Police Force. The last call was to Wilson, is aide de camp from Uganda, whom he asked to join him that night for a mission.

He also asked Wilson to prepare an update on their outstanding operations, and the current security schedules of targeted border countries on the other side of the Mediterranean Sea. Finally, he asked Wilson to book hotel reservations for three persons.

Jasmine has been avoiding top joints in Tripoli of late, but he intended to spend some quality time with his friends when they arrive. He was eager to catch up with the old times and all that he had missed in Oghara, Benin and their country Nigeria since he left. He also had a billion questions for Daba, concerning their two little families.

'After this assignment am out of Libya,' Jasmine reaffirmed, and he dressed up to go and see Kharig at the Spotlight.

CHAPTER 11

ANOTHER FALLEN STAR

Mena's health took a good turn after they joined Gyadhi's company, and the group benefitted from her charisma and humor.

One time they arrived at a remote village, in the environs of Sahba, where Gyadhi had stopped to pay a visit to a mechanic. The workshop was located in a remote area, yet, many long-distance drivers usually go there to have their engines and tires checked. The crew later spent the night at the house of the head mechanic KALLAH BAQI, who was also an acquaintance of Gyadhi.

As early as 8 am the next morning, Mena had managed to charm all the children around Mallam Baqi' house and beyond, giving them some local sweet which she had bought from a woman, who brought some for Baqi's wife.

She even tried to join in on a song that the children sang in the Arabic language with pleasure. It seemed like a popular song in the locality, because all of the children, including the smallest kids sang it word for word.

The gifts and the charm of the tall and beautiful African lady, really got the wards in the mood, and they started chasing after Mena, all over the place. They all had fun with cute grins on their faces, like they were playing with a friend they have known all their lives.

Mena on another occasion facilitated their easy passage during an encounter with the authorities at Houn. There she stunned the guards by responding in standard Arabic, when questions were directed at her crew.

She explained to the agents that, what Gyadhi the driver had told them was true, that she was the producer of an African film which is being shot at a location in Misrata, and that the rest of the passengers were actors, including the two local stars.

Mena told them that they were heading for the 15th century Misrata Castle, to join the larger film crew, to shoot some scenes at the popular landmark.

Gyadhi had anticipated the tight security in the area, and had suggested that the group should agree on a story to explain why they should be let through, in the event that they encountered unyielding security operatives. Mena had come up with the plan, with Victor providing information about the popular landmark in Misrata.

They were allowed to go through after a few questions, not just because of the accuracy by which Mena stated their direction, but also because of the manner in which she spoke. Arab men respect educated women, almost to a fault. They were supposed to ask for papers, but the officers did not.

The crew burst into laughter when Mena later explained to them what she told the Libyan security agents. They continued their journey up north at the next intersection, instead of going east towards Misrata, as Mena had claimed.

Mena had bugged Gyadhi all day at the front seat with questions about the desert, the people and the heat in the Sahara. She also overdid herself in convincing Gyadhi that the 'Film-Cast' explanation was the best plan.

So when the Libyan driver started explaining to the men in that direction, Mena immediately understood the format, and was prepared for the explanation. They were also fortunate that the area had experienced comparative peace since the turmoil which followed the 2011 ousting of the strongman of Libya. So the guards were not as stringent as may be found in other crises hotspot.

Mena had learnt to speak the Arabic language from her primary and secondary school days at Kano, in northern Nigeria, where Islamic and Arabic studies were compulsory subjects in schools.

Her father, a Catholic had operated a medium-sized rice mill in the ancient emirate, until he expanded to other locations in Nigeria, before establishing his business headquarters in Lagos.

Love without doubt, could be one of life's greatest motivators. It was at work to propel Mena, the rich and beautiful lady to leave the comfort of her wealthy home, to wallow in the Sahara Desert, where life was indeed wicked and unpleasant.

She had chosen this path for the solace of being in the company of the person that mattered most to her: Victor. Mena was convinced that she will make the same choice over and over again, and in another lifetime.

Currently, they have passed the Sahara Desert region, and were now going through the hills and plains, heading towards Bani Walid. They must endure this last huddle, before they will get to towns closer to the Mediterranean Sea, where the climate was moderate. It was at one of such locations that Gyadhi had said he will hand them over to another of Jasmine's cronies and be on his way, probably back into the desert.

'This stretch is where the dust storms are at their vilest,' Gyadhi said under a covered face, due to the severity of the weather, as he climbed the burnet of the lorry that morning to get some things checked. He was putting on a type of shades known in Nigeria as "Abacha glass" which was a gift from Jasmine.

Indeed, the weather was just as the desert maestro had predicted. This time around it was not only Mena that was affected, but all the other crew members as well, with the exception of Gyadhi and of course; his servants Musa and Abu, who did their best to provide the Nigerians succor.

The heat was intense and the air was dry, which made it extremely difficult for one to breathe. And in almost a day's drive, there was no settlement in sight where they could get some more refreshments. All they were left with was barren lands, dusty winds and the hot sun.

All of them were kitted in a similar fashion as the driver, with glassed on and keffiyehs covering their heads and necks, as they hid themselves as best as they could from the chaotic environment.

But then again, it was Mena that was most hit by the recent turn of events, and her condition this time around was worse than the last.

She could hardly breathe. Her face had become white, like she applied excess powder to it. Her lips were even whiter and hardened, like it was sunbaked. By nighttime her situation has become alarming that she could neither sit, eat, nor talk. And there was nowhere to get proper help, as the hours went by.

It became obvious that if she did not get immediate medical attention, something bad might happen. Worst still, was that nobody in the truck had any medical experience to intervene.

They all hoped and prayed that the amazing strength she had displayed throughout the course of the journey would see her through.

Gyadhi had estimated that they will arrive Bani Walid, by noontime the next day, where they will take her to a hospital.

Victor was worried by Mena's condition, and he too could not sleep that night, despite his own frail health. He held on to his "baby," as he used to call her.

'The Adekoko's will surely accuse me, and sue me for kidnapping their daughter, if they have not done so already,' Victor he imagined.

He was convinced that Mr. Adekoko will do everything possible to frustrate him, if he ever returned to Nigeria. Not only because he has the means to do so, but especially because Mena was his, and Mrs. Adekoko's treasure too.

But that was the least of his worries for now. All he wished for at the moment, was the resurrection of the best thing that has happened to him, and he was ready to deprive himself of sleep and be on alert for the slightest opportunity to be of help.

The next day, Mena's condition reached a point where all attention was now on her. Gyadhi had stopped driving, and had ordered his boys to erect a tent, so she could rest. She was in a desperate situation.

Victor has started crying uncontrollably, while Daba, Gyadhi and the rest looked on, as Mena struggled for her life taking a breath after every three seconds. They all knew that the end was inevitable for the precious African flower.

'Another star is set to fall after the Sahara crossing,' Gyadhi reflected.

'This one is of a unique kind, without any doubt,' He said in Arabic and folded his arms, thereby squeezing his jalabiya to his chest, as the rest of the garment tries to go off his body from the effect of the strong wind.

'While many who have fallen in the desert are mostly economic migrants, or refugees, this one is a victim of love.' Gyadhi said, this time in English, tainted by a native accent.

He had perceived that Mena was a sophisticated girl, by the way she talks and the manner which she carried herself. But now, she will join the millions of Africans who have lost their lives due to the implication of the meeting between Africa and Eura, many lifetimes ago.

Gyadhi had taken a liking to Mena since they joined his company, and was grief-stricken. He taught it unimaginable before now that he would feel this way over the demise of a migrant in the desert, after close to three score years on mother earth, and haven seen dozens of people die in the Sahara Desert.

He now believed in his heart that Mena was the chosen one to break the African curse, and lift the continent from the lengthy spell of hardship, to usher in an era of prosperity and a return to a time of abundance.

The wind was terrible that day, even when it was close to noontime. They all surrounded Mena under the tent, as she laid between Victor's laps and rested her head on his right bicep, while Victor used his spare hand to squeeze Mena to himself. He tried to protect her from the severe cold she had complained of, but now she was gasping for breath.

Mena finally gave up the ghost in the outskirts of Bani Walid. She was laid to rest in a cairn, by a hillside overlooking the town.

CHAPTER 12

MISSION TO AS ZAWIYAH

Before the meeting with Kharig that midnight, Jasmine paid quick visits to two Tripoli-based businessmen, who have ongoing projects with the Clique. His last port of call being the collection of a briefcase containing $1,000,000 in hard currency from MALLAM HUSSAINI, at the Mercato Di Tripoli. The money was part payment for a request for the supply of weapons. The trader was also a middleman between the Clique and a militant organization, operating in Libya.

'Let us go to the Spotlight,' Jasmine said, nudging Wilson with his left elbow from the passenger's seat. Wilson was glued to his phone, waiting for a software to finish downloading, when Jasmine entered the car. 'Okay boss,' he responded and paused the process. He then turned the car towards Garden Avenue, for a shortcut to their destination. Aside being a tech whiz kid, Wilson was also an excellent driver. Jasmine loved having him on the wheels, especially in these uncertain times in the country.

The Spotlight is a highbrow hotel in the middle of Tripoli, which members of the Clique find conducive for their rare meetings. Perhaps, because among the hotel's top shareholders was a purported Canadian investor, who had shipping interests in the Mediterranean Sea region. He was rumored to have ties with the Clique.

Jasmine reclined on the leather seat of the car, and felt troubled again, but he could not figure out what the problem was this time.

'Could it be because of this visit to Kharig?' He thought.

'The Boss has a message for you,' was the few words the Libyan had provided when he called him to confirm the appointment not long ago.

He has not heard from the Boss directly, in almost two years now. He remembered the last time he had a deal involving Mr. Rajab, the take-home pay was worthwhile. Yet, something in Kharig's voice just wasn't right, on the other side of the line.

Rumor also has it that The Islamist State of Libya and the Levant is planning a major offensive on the capital, thus bringing a gloom over Tripoli and affecting the general scheme of things.

These thoughts made Jasmine all the more anxious to reach the Spotlight, see Kharig, and know what it is the MIEN has to do this time. He was beginning to hate answering to calls, just like this one.

Over the last nine years in Libya Jasmine has directly executed over two hundred assignments for the Clique, including pushing hard drugs and transporting human cargos. In addition to marshalling other unpleasant missions for the organization.

Like one time, they were asked to deliver more than twenty teenage girls into a luxury ship, docked at a remote location off the coast of Tripoli.

He was livid the first time he was engaged to take delivery of such a consignment. The truck had been imported from neighboring Tunisia, so he was sent to clear it on behalf of the Clique. He succeeded by using his network of custom officials to secretly execute the clearance, only to find fifteen little girls between the ages of thirteen and sixteen, all dressed in black Hijabs and packed at the back of the medium sized van, like fish inside a sardine can. Their eyes riddled with fear, they were like frightened cats cuddled at the room' edge.

Surged by emotion, Jasmine slammed the door of the van and called the Clique's landline, which was marshaled by staff under the direct supervision of Kharig.

After about five rings, someone took the call at the other end. But before the person could say "hell...o," Jasmine started pouring out his frustration.

'What is the meaning of this?!' He yelled.

'*Am I now a child trafficker*?!' Jasmine screamed with rage, ignorant of the voice from the other end of the telephone. But the calm way the person said: "hello, hello" finally caught his attention. The voice is unmistakable: The boss was on the line.

'*Hello, Sir*,' Jasmine responded, and listened attentively.

'Jasmine, the man called in a British accent.

'Yes, Boss!' Jasmine replied again.

'No more questions,' Mifta Rajab said.

Piiiiinnn! The call ended.

The boss has spoken, what was left was for his orders to be carried out to the later.

Human trafficking is a dangerous business, and the psychological effect on perpetuators is immense. The business eats at one's soul.

Jasmine hated the human cargo aspect of his job, and undertook them only on direct orders from Mifta Rajab himself.

Reluctantly, he proceeded to organize the MIEN to facilitate the evacuation of the girls to an assigned location, with Wilson providing valuable information on safe entrance and escape routes, using some high-tech equipment.

The civil strife in Libya had become more intense since 2014, but it did not deter the

Clique's operations in and out of the country, due to the sophisticated modus operandi of the body.

'The secret is to lay low, Jasmine. And to make a move, only when necessary.

'That's the key to survival in this dirty trade,' Kharig would always say.

Thud, Jasmine has never had any issues with the authorities in Libya all these years, since he has been nurtured to become a master of impersonation. His identity on any given mission was determined by the plan, as directed by John Mountbatten, at the top of the administrative chain.

Jasmine has no permanent place of abode and was always on the move, within Libya and the Maghreb. His only weakness was perhaps, the rendezvous with Omon in Tripoli, mostly at the Pyramid. However, he takes the risk because the hotel was operated by trusted affiliates of the Clique.

He moved over to the bar inside the private section at the Spotlight, to get himself another shot of Remy Martin, as he waited for Kharig, deep into the night.

Jasmine had been informed that Kharig would be arriving late, through a note delivered by the barman. It was written by Kharig, in his usual bad writing, and it read: "*I will be late.*"

The notes weren't necessary, but Kharig likes writing them. He does so to practice the little English he had learnt in his early days, whilst as a student in Egypt, before he was expelled at Grade 5. His father had worked there as an expatriate medical doctor in the '50s.

After about two hours that seem like eternity, men on suit started pouring into the room, in a fashion that still made Kharig be in the middle. Although they all came in through the same door, one at a time.

'Jamin my boy!' Kharig said loudly, spreading his arms to hug Jasmine, who was seated on a long stool, at a side of the large room.

'Am sorry to keep you waiting this long, my boy.

'You know I got business all over the place,' the Libyan said, and led Jasmine to a nearby sofa. There the Linksman received the briefcase from the Recommended, put it on his laps and opened it. He scanned the content quickly, and handed it to one of his bodyguards.

'Even now, I don't have much time,' Kharig said again, and stood up from the circular chair they had settled on. He moved to where Jasmine was, took his left arm under his right armpit, and led him to one of the inner rooms at the secret bar.

After Jasmine had shut the door behind them, Kharig's expression changed all of a sudden, like he wasn't the cheery potbellied man just moments ago.

'How is the streets, my boy?' He asked feigning normality again, as he drew out a chair from a dining table to seat, but the look of worry in his eyes betrayed him.

'Nice, Boss.' Jasmin answered curtly, as he too drew out an opposite chair underneath the table, still puzzled about the reason behind the call, and Kharig's surprising change of countenance.

'I hear you have got your own connections across the country, they tell me,' the Libyan said, looking at Jasmine intently, from two swollen eye sockets.

He then took a long drink from the glass of water brought to him by an attendant, waited until he left, before reeling out the details of the mission to Jasmine.

'I spotted the industry in you since our first major job together at Benghazi, and you have never failed to deliver for us ever since.' He began.

'Perhaps, that is why the Boss has chosen you for this special mission, among all the agents at the Clique's disposal in the region. He said it is a major operation that must be executed with utmost precision.

'He also said to tell you that after this assignment you can disappear to Europe, or back to Nigeria, if that is what you want.' Kharig said.

Jasmine who had been listening attentively stood up and went back to the bar for another glass of cognac. He returned with a glass of water too, which he handed to Kharig, who was by now visibly shaking without any attempt to hide it.

'What do I need to do?' Jasmine asked, after a brief pause.

'The Boss needs you to get your MIEN on stand-by for a move,' Kharig said. It was the manner members of the Clique used to refer to the transportation of cargos, be it man, or materials.

'When is this move?' Jasmine asked Kharig, almost impatiently.

'You will get the details from the postman in the morning. But in the meantime, you get $10,000 take-off payment, and a balance of the same, when the deal is done.' Kharig said, and stretched his hands towards one of the bodyguards, who had just entered the room. The tough looking guy obliged, and placed a bundle of dollar notes on Kharig's palm, which he then passed on to Jasmine.

'This must be urgent,' Jasmine said, looking at the wad of cash in his hand.

As things are right now, the MIEN is probably the only reliable option available to the Boss, and he has total confidence in your capabilities.' Kharig noted.

Lately, Jasmine has been having the feeling that Tripoli was becoming sour; this encounter with Kharig was the confirmation he needed to clear his doubts. 'Something must be fishy at the top echelon of the Clique,' he also thought.

He took a quick drink from his glass, dropped it on the table and stood, as Kharig took his leave, with his guards taking the same formation they had come with.

CHAPTER 13

WANTED IN A STRANGE LAND

'We have been on the trail of this intercontinental criminal organization operating in the Mediterranean axis for several decades.' Agent Jake told members of the Joint Operations Team, JOT, comprising personnel of the International Criminal Police Organization and contingents from Libyan security and paramilitary organizations.

'Remember, our mission is targeted at those with ties to migration activities in North Africa. As you may well know, the current migration crises has led to the intensification of our effort to arrest the gangs aiding the exodus.

'Top on our list is this Englishman John Mountbatten A.K.A. Mifta Rajab, and his cronies known as the Clique.' Jake said, pointing to the picture on a wall to identify the suspect.

'The organization is said to operate in the fashion of the human body and John Mountbatten is the head, while others were mere stooges who did his bidding in the name of the Clique. He is currently wanted by the Libyan and Egyptian authorities for terrorism related offences and human trafficking charges. He has also been on INTERPOL's wanted list since the early 1982, but has escaped the agency's radar ever since.

'Not a handful of people in Libya could claim to have direct dealings with the man the international police has tagged: "THE GHOST OF NORTH AFRICA."

'John Mountbatten's antics have worked to his advantage for decades and has helped him to evade the authorities across the region.' Jake said.

Agent Jake Thomas, the Harvard graduate from Louisiana in the United States of America, assigned to seek the "Ghost" and crush the Clique, had come with a sophisticated profile. The Special agent had been excellent in his most recent project in South America, where he was reputed to have brought down the El Patron Brotherhood, who held sway from Chile, all the way to Florida, in the USA.

However, the task to bring the elusive Briton to Justice, since it was assigned to him in 2011, has not been as successful as the Latin America job.

He had toiled without much success to locate Mifta Rajab, talk less of arresting him. And some of his superiors at the headquarters were beginning to lose hope on his chances of succeeding.

His quarterly reports to the Command Center in Spain, in the past four years has been far from impressive, because the group whom he was assigned to apprehend existed only in their investigative intelligence, but not in real life.

The Clique has proven to be an influential, intelligence driven entity, which has mastered the art of migrating people, weapons and ammunition across North Africa, the Mediterranean region and sub-Saharan Africa.

Except for Mifta Rajab who was on the wanted list of over a dozen countries, and who was clearly identified as the leader of the Clique, the group operated in total secrecy and there was no single record of member's activities in police records in Libya. Perhaps, there were secret files in the possession of some chiefs in the nation's security apparatus, but even the adamant Jake, had almost doubted their existence.

'However, our breakthrough has come,' Jake announced to the team. At this point, many stopped taking notes, and they all focused their attention on Jake.

'We just received credible intelligence about a 2006 arrest of a suspicious cargo by the authorities at Benghazi. The information has it that the convey transporting the seized items to Tripoli for investigation was attacked at Sirt, by a group of young boys and girls, led by a young African migrant known as Jamin.

'The report has it that one of the attackers was killed in the operation, but the men succeeded in recovering the goods to their sender. Moreover, after a follow-up on available data, we discovered that John Mountbatten indeed, masterminded the hijack mission.

'We also have information concerning the goods which the Libyan authorities had intercepted; its origins from Ukraine in Europe and the intended destination in Niger Republic, in West Africa.' Jake concluded the profiling of the prime suspect, as well as the new suspects, and explained the modus operandi for the arrest of the Nigerian, and the final clampdown on the Clique and Mifta Rajab.

Jake carefully studied the records on the Benghazi hijack on his desk at the end of the meeting, after the participants had departed. He believed if he could get to the Nigerian, who led the attack at Sirt, his boss wouldn't be too far off.

***

A single loud knock on one's door at 5 am, was the signal for delivery of dispatches by the Clique's official postman. The man probably in his mid-40s would in his usual fashion, walk to room 69 at the Pyramid, knock once, and stand still by the door, like a Swiss Guard at the Vatican.

After the visit at the Spotlight, Jasmine had spent the remaining part of the night alone at the Pyramid, in expectation of what the postman was delivering that early morning.

'You have a mail,' he would say with a stern look, before handing the message over.

Jasmine had always wondered what the postman meant by that look, but has not bothered to push the issue. At least he was sure that the strange man is a member of the Clique else, he would not have lived to see the next day after delivering one of those dispatches.

The packages usually contained the minutest details and documents to execute a task, which could include forged international passports and identity cards when necessary. This assignment had all that.

Jasmine left the hotel a few hours after receiving the postman's message on "The Mission to As Zawiyah". He got to his car that morning still weighed down by hangover, and tossed the brown envelope containing the information on the passenger' seat, and drove to a nearby filling station to fill up his tank. Wilson had left after dropping him at the Spotlight some few hours back, and he wished he was around to be on the wheels again because of his present condition.

At the gas station he helped himself with the nozzle and quickly made the payments.

As he was about to open the door to get into the car a red Audi, with two occupants sped by, and they stared at him suspiciously.

Jasmine thought he had seen those faces before.

He got inside the car quickly, and adjusted the rear view mirror to take another look at the car that just zoomed by, to ensure his mind wasn't playing a fast one on him. He was almost certain he had seen the red Audi car recently. He was particularly sure because of the guy with the big black shades behind the wheels, and his companion with a steady sad look. 'Maybe it is déjà vu,' he pondered.

He started the car and headed towards the direction of Gharyan, for an approximately one hour twenty minutes' drive, to inspect a safe-house stipulated for the special delivery.

Meanwhile, Jasmine took his mind back to his calculations on some important tasks at hand, together with the latest assignment by the Clique which was activated immediately he opened the envelope. The mission turned out to be a one person target, as opposed to the transporting of multiple people, which gave Jasmin some sort of relief.

He had informed Wilson, who was on another mission, about the current job at hand. He had also given specific tasks to each of the MIEN regarding the assignment. His role was to coordinate the mission of getting the client out of the given location, and out of arms way.

But no fewer than 10 km on the road, the red car resurfaced, and overtook Jasmine, this time maneuvering awkwardly in front of his SUV, like the driver has gone berserk. The Audi later began to slow down, like its controller has finally decided to park it.

As he overtook the car, Jasmine could see the boys gesticulating in a manner that seemed like they were having an argument, with the sad one waving what looked like a pistol.

'However stupid these guys may seem, this is definitely a cause for concern.' Jasmine feared, as he took the next right turn in a hurry, and increased his speed. He intended to reconnect the highway at the next intersection, and hoped the awkward fellows were not using the same route. Now he was convinced he was being followed.

***

HOSNI and YUSUF were among several friends at their father's compound a few hours ago, where the boys in the area usually gather every Saturday after morning prayers. But the real men get to go to the backyard with the siblings to smoke hashish and cigarette, and talk about girls.

They are the two surviving sons of MALLAM MAHMUD, after the rebellious first son Marwan, left home when he was sixteen and was killed in a smuggling job at Sirt. A mission led by their current bait, whom their father had sworn revenge on.

The wealthy and influential Mallam Mahmud, was a top ranking police officer before his retirement and still had his connections in the Libyan Police authority. It was one of his contacts that brought in the lead on Jasmine, whom the two crack-heads are currently monitoring.

Their father had instructed them to track Jasmine down to a location, so that men would be sent to pick him up at night. Mr. Mahmud wanted him interrogated, before his execution.

But Hosni's state of mind wasn't in the right place, as he almost shot the target. It was Yusuf who intervened, and cautioned that they should stick to the plan and remain on a low key until Jasmine's hideouts were determined.

Meanwhile, the incident alerted Jasmine to the heightened danger at hand, but he proceeded with his current mission nonetheless. He resolved to relocate Omon to yet another safe place, before they would leave Libya for good.

'Yes, that's what I'll do,' he soliloquized.

Jasmine pressed his foot on the throttle, bringing the car to full speed, as he headed for Gharyan.

CHAPTER 14

THE REUNION

LIFE IS COMPLICATED, LIFE IS SIMPLE

Life is complicated, yet simple;
What goes around, comes around
Don't plant plantain, and expect cocoyam.
Life is lopsided: abundance here, lack there
Hot here, cold there.
Life is love and pain, highs and lows
We live, grow old and die
Whether in Oghara, or Oslo.
Life simply regenerates, and moves on.
Between simple and complicated,
Life is somewhere in the middle.
***

Victor finished putting his thoughts into writing, just as they reached the outskirts of Tripoli. He folded the paper he wrote on into a neat square and kept it in his pocket. He was not sure whether to call it a poem, or a dirge, but he has made many of such writings. They mostly bothered on his thoughts, his worries, difficulties in his country, and in sub-Saharan Africa generally. He writes, whenever he was going through a tough time.

Victor had also written a passionate later to the Adekoko's, which he hoped Jasmine would help him send to Nigeria, when they get to Tripoli. He picked up his bag to catch up with Daba, who was saying farewell to Gyadhi. He took his turn to hug the benevolent Libyan, who was standing by his truck.

He also followed Daba to give Abu and Umar solid handshakes, as they stood at the rear of the truck emotionless. The boys then turned, and took quick steps to join a thick black man, positioned at the driver's seat of a massive, black jeep waiting for them.

The travelers had arrived a day short of schedule, due to the passing of Mena, and her mourning by the group. The elements had mourned her as well, evidenced by the intensity of the sandstorms which characterized the last parts of their journey, after she gave up the ghost.

As a result of the delays Gyadhi, who had thought to join them to see Jasmine in Tripoli, was unable to fulfil his promise. Instead, he went to his house in the city to see his family, whom he had planned to take back with him to Al Qatron, due to the palpable tension in Tripoli. He had already discussed with Wilson about the demise of Mena.

'My name is Wilson,' the chubby guy who had come out of the car said, and stretched out both his large hands to welcome the emigrants, with a forceful handshake.

'Welcome to Libya.

'Congratulations.

'Congratulations,' Wilson said again, while maintaining a beam, like the boys had just won a prize for a cross-country competition across the Sahara Desert.

Daba and Victor were at a loss on how to respond to the charged felicitations from the stranger, who was talking with the all too familiar East African accent. The kind you hear from a movie about Idi Amin.

'Thank you.'

'Thank you.' Daba barely muttered to Wilson's two hearty 'congratulations!'

He did not want to offend the stranger taking them to Jasmine, all too soon.

Inside the SUV, Daba and Victor were not in the mood for any kind of talk, after such a long and tortuous journey. Especially after the sorrow which overtook them, since they lost Mena at Bani Walid.

They just sat quietly, Daba at the front seat, while Victor was at the back seat of the rather comfortable car, with perfect air conditioning system. But even that was not enough to take away their grief, especially Victor. He had only said a few words since Mena gave up the ghost, and half of it was delivered as soliloquy.

Wilson understood what they have been through, and decided to let them be.

But he did not feel pity for them.

In fact, he meant it when he saluted them, because anyone who had survived the journey across the Sahara Desert, was indeed worth celebrating.

He had embarked on the adventure himself, many years ago and has been too cowardly to take the same route back home, after he was stranded in Libya in 2006. Then, he had ran out of money to pay for the deadly boat ride across the Mediterranean Sea, to his destination in Italy.

However, when he came in contact with Jasmine, things changed for him positively. But he too, like the Nigerian, has been stuck right between the Sahara and the Mediterranean obstacles, since they left home.

Wilson dusted himself off those depressing thoughts. He checked on the passenger on his right side, and the other at the back seat, through the rear view mirror and said: ‘I’ll take you guys to Jasmine now.’

He glided the vehicle off the dusty road to the tarred portion, without taking his foot off the throttle and headed to mainland Tripoli.

***

FATIMA had wanted to run away from her purported "aunties," at the large waiting room of the Modern Girls School in As Zawiyah, until they showed her the red bracelet.

'Who are you people?' She asked Aisha and Amina, studying their body movement carefully, to know if there was still need to alert the authorities.

'We don't have much time,' Aisha hushed, and stretched a short note to her with the brief content:

"THEY CARE. LOVE."

She instantly recognized her father's handwriting on the note, it corroborated the RED BRACELET CODE, which signaled imminent danger.

'What do you want me to do?' Fatima asked the Somali sisters, this time with a concerned look.

'There is no excuse we can give the school authorities that will make them allow us to take you.' Amina said, as she rolled her eyes around the school premises, through the large windows in the visitors' lounge.

'Fatima, you have to find a way around that side of the fence, through those short trees.' She pointed, using her eyes to direct the girl.

'We will wait for you by the side of the road.

'Leave everything behind,' she concluded, and headed for the security desk to sign out the visitation form, as Aisha went straight ahead to get their car.

Fatima did as she was told, and rendezvoused with the two ladies in less than ten minutes.

As they drove past, they saw two black SUVs at the school gate, with one man saying to the personnel at the entrance: 'We are here for Fatima.'

This made the sixteen year old to dock even better at the back seat of the Nissan car of her rescuers.

***

Jasmine has been working around the clock for the past forty-eight hours, and has settled Omon into a new hiding place. This time, it was a condo he had bought secretly in Tripoli, with a pseudonym.

'Enough of the secrets, Jasmine,' was the attack from his girlfriend, when he returned from another trip to Gharyan.

'It is high time your told me what is going on,' Omon said with rage, when he entered the living room.

She has not left the place all day, after Jasmine had pleaded with her to be on low key with him in the interim.

'I promise, it will all be over real soon, babe.' Jasmine tried to sweet-talk Omon, but it was in vain, as she shrugged off his hands from her shoulders.

'After a few more appointments in the next few days, all will be settled for us to leave.' He said to the angry lady, who was yet to forgive him for abandoning her in the lonely apartment in the first instance, not to talk of more appointments.

'My friends have arrived and I have to...'

'Just go!' Omon shouted at him, before he could finish what he was about to say.

'It will only take a few...'

'Go, Jasmine!' Omon fired again, as she stepped away from where he was, and swiftly went to lock herself in a nearby room.

The couple have had this kind of argument a million times before, due to Jasmines secretive ways.

Although Omon has a clue about what he does for a living, she was frustrated that Jasmine would never say the words, despite his claim of unconditional love for her.

Jasmine too, understood her frustration and respected her wish to be alone at the moment, so he left the condo. He knew he was protecting her by not revealing information regarding his dealings with the Clique, but doesn't know how to make her understand his intentions.

Jasmine drove to the Municipal Beach, his favorite place for relaxation, whenever he was overwhelmed by stress. The place was a stone throw away from the condo. There he took a long seep from the glass of Fanta, which was served chilled and reclined on a long chair facing the waters.

He was having what he called his "stress therapy," just by watching the waves and the picturesque, clear blue skies of the once peaceful country. He called it his "me-me time," which amused Omon whenever he said the words.

Today he was not there for the relaxation alone, but had planned the public place as his meeting point with his friends.

Jasmine did a check on his remaining agendas for the day, to calculate how to execute them. The safe house at Gharyan had been the ideal place to keep Fatima, pending a transfer to a new location that will be made known to him the next day.

In the meantime, Omar the Algerian, was acting as the new occupant of the newly refurbished, four room apartment at Gharyan, with Aisha and Amina his fake wives.

Haggi, the Somali and the three Libyans: Abdo, Aziz and Mustafa, have mounted watch at the place either as drivers, gardeners or cooks, including the late Marwan Mahmud's replacement BELLO, the Senegalese. Luckily, the client was cooperating.

His focus was now to welcome and facilitate the smooth transition of his friends across the Mediterranean Sea to nearby Italy, where he had perfected plans with agents there, to take Daba and Victor to Germany.

Their arrival had also got him thinking a lot about his days in ‘O-land,’ as the boys usually referred to Oghara, their hometown in Delta State, Southern Nigeria.

Jasmine grew up without the support of a father he never knew, and only had a mother, who did not complete secondary school, to fend for him. He had endured hardship from an early age, which had sharpened his survival instinct, and made him a hardcore hustler.

He and Daba, his childhood neighbor and best friend, started skipping school to do menial jobs, whilst as little children, following the death of the latter’s father, JESSE.

For a long time they were under the employ of Lalalolo, a famous farmer in Oghara, as apprentices. He taught them how to tap rubber from rubber trees, using tapping knife and other equipment. He also taught them how to cultivate and nurture different tree types.

Soon they became experts at tapping rubber that the old farmer would leave them in one of his plantations, and go to another one for the day’s job.

Jasmine and Daba would go to the farm after school to tap like two monkeys on trees, till the evening time.

They were able to make a combined total of N80 weekly for their hard labor. It was the money the boys took home to play at being little daddies for their mummies.

They had taken the desperate measure to escape the hardship they endured as children, and to support their homes. By their teenage years they have begun to enjoy making money on their own.

They enjoyed the freedom that came with their status, as providers at home. They also loved having constant money in their pockets to cater for their little needs, especially those night-outs in the village center called “Garage”.

The Garage in O-Land is not a garage per say, but the busiest junction in the village, especially at night. It is the place where they bought *suya* (roasted cow meat) from MALLAM GARUBA, to entice the young girls in Oghara, famous for their rare beauty.

They attended lots of late night burials which were common in the community in those days, and had great fun chasing after damsels all through the night. They also picked up a few vices, like smoking their first cigarette at the age of fifteen.

So, with the love of money and the power it yields, together with the love their mothers showered on them out of share respect for their guts, the boys grew up to become extremely confident young men, and inseparable money chasers.

One time they joined a free bus ride from Oghara to a massive church crusade, held at the open field of the Mini stadium of the University of Benin, in Benin City. There they had hoped to meet young ladies who were known to be enthusiasts of such activities.

He recollected they were so impressed with the structures and people around the campus on that occasion. That was when Daba had come up with the suggestion that they should attempt to gain admission into the Great UNIBEN, as the institution was popularly known.

He had eagerly obliged and suggested that they should go and see Victor, the smartest guy they knew back home, for tips on how to go about their mission.

'We are going to open a barbing saloon somewhere around that beautiful campus, and style those students for their money!' He had enthused.

'But we only just started learning the skills at SIMEON's saloon, Daba had cautioned.

'Don't worry Dabs,' he had assured his friend, throwing one of his arm over his shoulders.

'There is nothing we cannot fix.' He said, as they went to seek Victor, upon their return from the crusade.

Their expert himself was an admission seeker. Victor had missed out on getting into the university, for the sheer reason that he had not been able to amass the N700 needed to acquire the JAMB form, three years after they graduated from Oghara Secondary School, OSS.

They were aware of the difficulties in passing the Joint Admission and Matriculation Board entrance examination, notoriously called "JAMB," which was a prerequisite for gaining admission into Nigerian universities. They have also heard of the financial commitment needed for a university education in Nigeria. But they were not deterred. That year they registered and took the exam, alongside Victor who they supported with registration fees, and all of them made it.

In their first two years at the university, He and Daba's focus was to meet as much girls as possible, and not necessarily about and the courses they were studying, or what great scholars they wanted to become.

For Jasmine, it was an opportunity to belong among other people. Like in the primary and secondary school days, where he made lots of friends. He had longed for those old times again, deep down in his consciousness.

At home their mothers had expressed mixed feeling of excitement and worry, as shown on their faces when the boys broke the news to them. Both of them Kikki Daba's mum, and Omatie Jasmine's mum, were at the local parish when the boys presented their admission letters to them, after the evening mass.

'So… how are you boys going to afford the huge amount they say, they pay in that kind of school?' Omatie, bravely asked, after a long pause.

'You know our….' Omate and Kikki were about to say simultaneously, before the boys cut in. They told the women not to worry, that they've got everything covered.

Soon they started schooling at the Federal University of Benin, which was not too far from Oghara. Daba chose to study Agricultural Science, while Jasmine who lacked options at the time copied Victor to read International Studies and Diplomacy. He had also opted for the course partly due to his bewilderment of how the world and humans came to be, and how the nations are coexisting.

They had made their choices after Victor had explained the different courses they were eligible for, while helping them to fill the admission registration forms in line with their individual interests.

The hustlers quickly set up a makeshift salon, at the back entrance of the campus, and in no time mastered the art of hair-cutting. Within a short period, their little enterprise blossomed from a tiny barbershop to a modest saloon, after they relocated to one of the business shops inside campus. They were so good at the job that the enterprise became a sprawling business. Jasmine alone made over two hundred thousand naira in savings upon graduation.

That was the money he used to launch his adventure to Eldorado without his friend Daba, who had chosen a five-year course, and had a year left to graduate. Something they had skipped when they were filling out the application forms. Thus, the best of pals have been separated for a whole nine years now.

Jasmine was excited about the prospect of their reunion, but was also exhausted due to stress and lack of proper sleep. He decided to take a nap at the beach, under a large, green canopy, as he waited for Wilson and his friends to arrive.

***

The situation was the same with Daba, who sat quietly at the front seat of the SUV, and ruminated on how far he has come since he left home.

He was thankful that they have succeeded in getting past the Sahara obstacle. So he braced himself for the other aspect of the journey, which was crossing the Mediterranean Sea.

For Daba, the thought of seeing Jasmine again brought a tinge of excitement, despite the difficulties dealing with the painful demise of Mena, and the physical and mental effects of the challenging experience across the Sahara Desert.

He was happy that he will get to see his friend again, after many years apart. He and Jasmine had lived like twins from different mothers. They ate together in one plate for many years, and shared the same piece of meat, or fish as the case may be. Sometimes all they would have as protein in their food, would be a quarter of a piece of fish to share, or a small piece of meat, after their mothers have taken their share.

Back in primary school MAMA KONO's food was their favorite. He and Jasmine would take from the little money they had, to get a delicious plate of rice and egg from her, which they ate together. Sometimes they added fifty kobo beans, or yam to the order, which was their perfect combination.

He remembered how mama Kono maximized the absence of a free lunch program for primary school pupils back then, to create a thriving enterprise at a corner of the public school. There she ripped the children off with menus like, a handful of rice and a quarter of an egg, for two naira. One naira for the rice and stew, and the other for the quarter of an egg.

Those days, it was a taboo for children to eat whole eggs by themselves. And any child caught doing so was branded an aspiring thief, and could face a day's punishment for such an offence.

Only a handful of students back then could afford what Mama Kono had to offer, talk less of the full menu.

Most times, the children who could not afford to buy her food would gather around Mama Kono's little kiosk at break time, to be on the lookout for their relatives, friends, neighbors or anyone they know, to beg for a pinch of rice or beans. Some desperate ones among them even begged randomly, and go after leftovers at the stand.

They usually do not beg for eggs, meat or fish, because they knew that the little piece of protein was the exclusive preserve of the person who bought the food. They would plead: *'eee, kevwe na!'*

An appeal in Urhobo language which meant, 'please, give me some.'

It was a common chant around Mama Kono's kiosk, during break time at Okome Primary School.

To scare away the beggars those days Dafinone, Mama Kono's favorite customer, would buy his best combination of rice and beans and one egg, and would publicly spit on it. He would then mix it up with his bare hand, before he would start eating. This method was his strategy to deter any would be beggars.

Only OTOR, the chief of the beggars still accepted food in that condition. But he avoided begging D1 for food, because of his hostile nature.

Thinking of it now, Daba had a doubt if Mama Kono's cooking was that great, but he remembered back then, it was definitely the bomb.

He also remembered that their mothers, just like many parents those days, do not encourage their wards to patronize these extra-home meals. And of course, never gave them any money for such frivolities.

Therefore, Mama Kono's meals were reserved for the rich kids, spoilt brats and home thieves. It was only after resumption from holidays like Christmas and New Year celebrations, that some children could afford her food. Many of the pupils literally saved the little money they gathered throughout the holidays, for a piece of her sweet rice and stew, with a quarter of an egg. And of course, she freely accepted money from those suspected of stealing from home, and treated their dealings with utmost confidentiality.

Daba found some of his reminiscing amusing, as they drove through a quiet road leading to the Municipal beach, where Wilson had mentioned they would meet Jasmine. He was almost certain his best friend was having similar reflections, where he was.

After a few minutes' drive they finally got to the beach, and Jasmine was there at the entrance to receive them.

Their reunion did not turn out to be spectacular as they had anticipated, because Mena's demise brought a new perspective to the hunt for paradise for Daba and Victor.

They wore long faces despite their best efforts to come out of their gloominess, to see their friend again. They just had long hugs and consoled each other, before Jasmine led them to a restaurant at the beachside, to have some food and drinks.

Wilson left immediately after the meals to take care of other business, while Jasmine took the boys to his condo to freshen up. He also bought fast-food for Omon, and some kilograms of roasted goat meat to the apartment.

They did not go out that evening due to news of the intensity of the crises at the outskirts of the capital, so they all spent the rest of the day at the penthouse.

Later in the evening, Jasmine provided two bottles of Jack Daniel's to lighten up the mood. And soon, they were reliving stories of old times. Their voices became louder and louder, as they drank with zeal.

Omon was enjoying the special Libyan delicacy of roasted goat meat and vegetables, which they had brought, and watched the two best friends chat away, with Victor in a world of his own. He rarely took a piece of meat from the large bowl on the table, but he was heavy on the booze. Even now his countenance has changed, as the effect of the cognac was kicking in. He was having too much of it.

Although Libya was one of the countries where the sale of alcohol was prohibited, yet, Jasmine has always had access to the commodity from the black-market.

Moreover, that evening alcohol was of the essence, because many men from the Niger Delta region of Nigeria were gathered in one place, so there was need to drink to the success of their future endeavors. The drinking and chattering went on until one after the other, each of them fell asleep at the spot they found themselves that night.

CHAPTER 15

THE CALL

The ring tone from the Nokia phone at 3am was loud, and the noise shook Jasmine out of sleep. He quickly removed the thick duvet from his legs and used it to cover Omon who was fast asleep, despite the noise from the alarm. He doesn't make calls around her, no matter what time it was, so he went to the balcony to answer the call.

The number was unknown to him, but the hour of call was almost unmistakable, it was the time of the day one could get a call from the "Ghost of North Africa". He pressed the green button, on the bottom-left corner of the screen and listened. A few seconds passed before someone spoke:

'Hello, Jasmine,' was the familiar voice from the other end of the telephone.

'Hello, Boss.' Jasmine responded, and listened, in anticipation of a directive.

He was always overwhelmed whenever he was contacted by Mifta Rajab directly. Maybe it was out of appreciation and respect for the man who rescued him, when he was at his lowest ebb, or, for the endorsement of his RECOMMENDED status in the organization.

He had noticed the striking resemblance between the girl he was rescuing and the boss. So, the unusual call after he had already received the brief on the assignment was not out of place.

The situation had proven that blood, was indeed thicker than water. John Mountbatten uncharacteristically went on to ask Jasmine about the MIEN's execution of the current mission, and about the safety of his daughter, Fatima.

'It turned out there are several forces after my daughter.' Mifta Rajab said on the other end.

'I hear INTERPOL has also intensified its chase on the Clique, and are now targeting my daughter too, all in a bid to get me.' He said.

The Briton had earlier gotten the intelligence that As Zawiyah, at the outskirts of Tripoli was on the verge of an attack, by loyalists of the late military ruler.

Fatima's school in North-western As Zawiyah, was identified as one of the target locations in the town. The place had hitherto been a haven for girl child education.

John Mountbatten has not only succeeded in evading the authorities in Libya all these years, but had also managed to keep a family with his Libyan wife AMIRA, whom he married at a small ceremony presided over by the late Hamuz

Mohammed himself. The union had produced Fatima, their only daughter, after many years of childlessness.

He cherished Fatima and wanted the best for her. So he had sent her to As Zawiyah, where she was training to become a nurse. He took her there because of the relatively modest level of security at the institution. Indeed, the area had not experienced any major incidents since the war, until now. Thus the early move to have Fatima evacuated from the school.

'The operations of the Clique is suspended as of this moment,' John said, after a brief pause.

'Noted, Sir.' Jasmine responded, and kept on listening.

'You too Jasmine must be on the lookout,' John Mountbatten cautioned.

'Your name is constantly being mentioned across our intelligence surveillance network,' he said.

'Deliver her to the location on the note in front of your door, then we'll talk.

'And, Jasmine, be safe.' John Mountbatten concluded. And ended the call.

The safety of his daughter depended on the level of timeliness and precision by the MIEN, in evacuating her from the safe house to her flight. The Ghost was troubled.

After the call Jasmine hurriedly went to open the front door of the luxury apartment, and retrieved the small white envelop he found on the floor. Inside the envelope was a small white paper with the message:

"GET HER ON THE 11:15AM FLIGHT TO TUNIS, AT THE MITIGA INTERNATIONAL AIRPORT, THE DAY AFTER TOMMOROW.

"EXTREME CAUTION NEEDED. COAST, NOT CLEAR."

Jasmine quickly discarded the message after memorizing the content, using a lighter to burn the small piece of paper. He was overwhelmed by the intensity, and importance of his current schedules. He found it even more difficult to sleep after the call. He used the time at the balcony to contemplate his agendas in the next 48 hours.

The easy decision would have been to incorporate his friends into the MIEN, and make them rich men overnight. But his conscience would not allow him. They say all adults have got to make their own decisions, but this was one choice he would not even allow his friends to make for themselves.

He had resolved to facilitate their easy transition through the Mediterranean Sea to Europe, and get on with his life.

Being on INTERPOL's wanted list, as Khariq had informed him recently was another reason he could not sleep. Not to mention the thought of other unknown enemies, including rivals of the Clique, whom he was told also want his head chopped off.

He began to update the MIEN in active duty on the mission focus, in line with the new directive from Mifta Rajab. He sent a message to Wilson, and another to the fake polygamous home in Gharyan. He then switched off his phone and returned to the bed to try and sleep away the pains from his banging headache.

Jasmine was completely unaware that an INTERPOL agent has been monitoring his movement for some days now. And that the agency has got to know about the disappearance of John Mountbatten's daughter and were mobilizing to identify her location.

CHAPTER 16

JAMIN AT WORK

Daba and Victor were no ordinary migrants else, at this stage of the journey their agent in Tripoli, would have driven them to a shanty for intending crossers. There their phones would have been taken from them, while other unnecessary items would be discarded. They would have been kept there for days, or weeks depending on the individual travel arrangements of the emigrants.

Environmental factors, such as the weather in the Mediterranean Sea, and security settlements can also determine how long a migrant could be kept at those safe houses.

To take Daba and Victor across to Italy, Jasmine had contracted WALID EMAD, an ex-official of the Libyan Coast guard, LCG. He was the best in arranging durable floating vessels to ferry clients through the murky waters of the Mediterranean Sea, to shores in Italy.

Walid understands the waters of the Mediterranean Sea like the back of his hand, and maximizes the July and August window to release his clients to the sea, usually by themselves. He holds the trademark of never losing a customer he was contracted to deliver, across the waters to Europe.

What he does, was to teach one of the migrants how to operate the motor of the raft, and how to use the compass. In addition to providing them with a Thuraya mobile phone, to make an emergency call to the European Authorities, when they reach the other end of the Mediterranean Sea.

He had been dismissed from service for taking a bribe, and had become very poor. Until he discovered his new calling in the thriving illegal migration sector in Libya.

Jasmine had provided the bribe on behalf of the Clique, and it was he too, who had supported Walid to get back on his feet when things were tough.

It was the Nigerian who also spotted Walid's prospects in the Mediterranean crossing business.

He had used his service many times, too. So he went to downtown Tripoli to seek his expertise one last time.

He walked past a cluster of shops off Rachid Street to Walid's house, where there were outlets for the sale of cheap Turkish-made guns and bullets.

'Everyone in Libya has got a gun these days,' Jasmine thought as he walked by, thinking the trend has reflected in the expansion of the arms market, since the last time he visited.

'Anyone, with anything that floats is now an agent.' Walid had lamented in his sitting room, with an expensive couch.

'The situation in Syria has intensified the migration crises, leading to the increasing number of the wannabe migrant's agents you identified.' Jasmine also observed.

'Yes, I agree,' the Ex-Coastguard said.

'But I could have guaranteed the safe transit of every single one of those migrants to Europe,' he boasted.

'The quacks need to pay more attention to the Sea; that is all!' He stressed.

'Overloading is another problem too,' Walid also decried.

He was frustrated by the de-marketing of his beloved trade by recent tragedies involving African migrants, crossing the Mediterranean Sea.

'You do not send people to sea without the proper knowledge and tools.' He added to the complaints. Walid was loquacious as ever.

However, Jasmine agreed with his observations about the goings on in the business of crossing migrants to Europe from Libya. That was why he had visited to give Walid the balance of the transaction, for the crossing of his friends to Italy.

Jasmine was not taking any chances, and had planned the best travelling arrangement for Daba and Victor known as, "THE SYRIAN TREATMENT".

The Syrian Treatment entailed a migration price-tag system used by agents to select boats to transport their clients to Europe, according to a structure where race and color were key determinants.

In such arrangements, the Syrian emigrants were made to pay the highest fee of $2500, and were provided boats in good condition, for their crossover to Europe. The next category are Libyans and other North Africans immigrating to Europe. People in this category were charged up to $1500 for the same journey, but were given a similar treatment to those offered the Syrians.

The African migrants were prioritized at the lowest rung in the system. And were meant to pay $800-$1000, to occupy positions on inflatable rafts, or dinghies for the journey across the Mediterranean Sea.

Jasmine hated the arrangement, but there was little he could do about it. He left Walid's house that afternoon desperate to put an end to all the activities he has been involved with, in the country. He also hoped it would be the last time he would have to make these kind of arrangements.

***

Jasmine has been receiving reports from the MIEN at Gharyan, about the spotting of strange faces in the area.

Abdo and Haggi, had seen a well-dressed man and a lady, come very close to the walls fencing the residence and even took a few peeps into the house, while pretending to be local officials.

Aziz and Bello also heard some men ask questions about a missing young girl, while they were at the filling station to get petrol for their two SUV's, ahead of the transfer the next day. Mustafa too, said he noticed some men loitering the quiet road leading to the compound, on his way back from an errand.

Also, the fake husband Omar and his not-real wives Amina and Aisha say, the authorities have made routine visits to the house for random questioning.

'Have they discovered our location, yet?' Jasmine asked Wilson for updates, whilst on the phone, as he headed back to the condo after the day's work.

'That is the last piece of the puzzle the police, and a Joint Task Force are trying to put together.

'The girls did a neat job during the evacuation at As Zawiyah,' Wilson who was monitoring ongoing security communications, reported to Jasmine.

He was currently on the servers of the police, the military and two major militant forces in the country. He was on the lookout for any mentioning of “Famita,” or “Jasmine,” to anticipate and preempt their moves.

‘At this moment nothing is sure, though. Everything is going on at a really fast pace.

‘You and the boss are now too famous on the channels I listen to,’ He said

‘We must round off all that we are doing and stay out of the radar for the meantime.’ Wilson cautioned.

‘I agree.’ Jasmine responded, and ended the call.

The meeting with Walid and the final payment to the Ex-Coastguard, was the last in his schedule for that day. He had also made arrangements for the secret evacuation of Fatima from the compound at Gharyan.

What was left, was for him to escort his buddies to the boat, and Fatima to her plane the next day. Then he and Omon would vanish out of Libya for good.

CHAPTER 17

THE DEPARTURE

Africans do not express emotions freely. It showed in the way Jasmine and Daba said their goodbyes, as the boys got set to depart for the last phase, and the aquatic section of their journey to Europe.

They just shook hands, and tapped each other's upper right arm with their left hands, and looked into each other's eyes only for a nanosecond.

Jasmine did the same thing to Victor, but the bereaved held his hand in a steady grip, and then hugged him. Although he had not said much since their arrival, he looked Jasmine straight in the eyes and said: 'thank you for everything,' in a defeated, but calm voice.

'You are welcome, bro.' Jasmine replied, while tapping his shoulders, after they shared an awkward hug.

Jasmine broke the silence after what seemed like lengthy seconds and said: 'I'll call,' to no one in particular. Then he left the side of the boat.

The vessel was supposed to have left by 5am, but there was a delay due to complaints by some passengers, about the inclusion of Africans in their vessel. Walid had pleaded with them all morning to no avail, until he threatened to refund their monies, before they soft pedaled, and the issue was finally resolved.

Now, it was almost 6am and Jasmine was in a hurry to leave to join Omon and Wilson at the latest hideout. He also wanted to personally coordinate the safe transportation of Fatima to her flight to Tunisia, later at 11.15am.

Walid meanwhile, was embarrassed by the whole scene, which had happened in front of his favorite patron. So he followed Jasmine who was leaving the beachside and spoke sporadically into his ears, as the client took quick steps away from him.

'Everything will be fine, Jamin.' He pleaded.

'They will get to Italy safely.' He assured him, but Jasmine was not in the mood for an explanation, and kept on walking until he outpaced Walid.

He was fed up with the treatment of Africans by some Arabs. He was very angry about what had just happened and felt he had truly seen enough.

He had done all he could to help his friends achieve their dreams. Although inwardly, he doesn't fancy the idea of the macabre journey from mainland Africa to Europe anymore. He wished he could make them change their minds and join him back to Nigeria.

Meanwhile, Daba stood on the boat to take perhaps, one last look at his childhood friend. Despite shouts to come back inside from FADI, the appointed captain of the boat. Daba knew that his standing on the boat would affect the balance of the vessel, and make it to wobble, but he had to do what he did.

His expression suddenly changed from one of reverie to worry, as he saw Jasmine took to his heels. He also noticed about five men, some with guns giving him a hot pursuit from another direction. Now his friend was racing towards the alternate exit, away from the main entrance of the beach.

'Jasmine is in trouble!' Daba exclaimed. Victor immediately joined him on top of the boat to see what was happening, to the angst of the supposed captain and many passengers in the boat. They both instinctively jumped into the water, swam out of it, and ran towards the direction that Jasmine was heading.

***

Agent Jake captured the whole drama from his binocular, a few meters away from the action.

'What is going on here?' he said out loud, as he watched Jasmine took to his heels, like he had suddenly gone mad. He removed his dark shades from his eyes, and observed as his target leapt from the pier unto a small boat, jumping from one to the other, and heading towards the beach's second exit.

Just behind him, the INTERPOL agent saw the two black guys he was yet to identify, jump out of their boat and ran towards Jasmine. At the same time, he saw some young men who looked like locals, chase after the suspect. One of them on dark shades, with a pistol had even started shooting, to Jake's bewilderment.

The INTERPOL agent realized that the valuable suspect was in danger, and he had to make a move. And fast.

He pressed his right foot on the throttle, after the maneuver with the gear and his left leg, and twisted the minivan towards EXIT B. Thus creating another scene, with the way he handled the vehicle, and the loud screeching sound it made.

Soon Daba and Victor kept pace with Jasmine, jumping, running and dodging bullets as he did, in the middle of rapid firing by the assailants.

Fortunately, a black SUV with Omon at the passenger's seat screeched in front of the Nigerians, and came to a wild halt. They jumped inside with Wilson who drove shouting: 'Get in! Get in!! Get in!!!'

It had all happened in a flash.

'The men after you are relatives of Marwan.' Wilson informed Jasmine, with eyes focused on the road, as he drove in top speed.

'I got the information that their father had declared revenge on you,' he said.

'One of them had mentioned on the telephone that their squad has got eyes on you, and were about to take you, that's why we had to come here to get you.' Wilson explained.

Jasmine was shocked beyond words because of the revelations by Wilson, but he was rather angry with his friends who had followed him, instead of being on their way to Italy.

'Why did you follow me?!' He screamed.

They were still panting at the back seat of the car, with Jasmin in the middle.

'Why did you leave the boat?!' Jasmine shouted again in frustration, and clasped his head with his hands.

'Why?!' He cried out again.

All the while, Omon who was panicking kept on looking all over Jasmine's body, to check if he was shot.

She had insisted on coming with Wilson, after the Ugandan mentioned at the motel, that her man was in imminent danger. They had left Fatima there, with a promise to return as soon as possible.

***

The lodge was located at a quiet town in the southern fringes of Tripoli. The distance between the new hideout and the airport, was just a ten minutes' drive.

Not long after they returned to the guesthouse where Fatima was, Wilson received news about an incident at the safe house at Gharyan. He stood up, listen attentively to something from his earpiece and announced:

'A joint Taskforce just raided the compound at Gharyan. All the MIEN there have been arrested,' Wilson said.

Now, he too was panicking.

Jasmine had instructed that the MIEN should stay behind at the residence, to make everything seem normal, after he had evacuated Fatima from the place the night before. The others were to leave the shelter, only after Fatima was out of the country.

Jasmine had escorted Fatima through a vast olive tree plantation in the dark, to a location where Wilson waited for them. That was how they succeeded out of Gharyan unnoticed, and he took her to the inn where he had also relocated Omon to. That same night, he left the girls at the lodge and went to the condo to join Daba and Victor, to spend their last night in Libya together.

'We will leave at eleven o'clock, on the dot.' Jasmine announced to the others, after a quiet spell inside the room. They have been stunned by the news of the arrest of the MIEN at Gharyan.

'I and Omon had booked a flight for Ghana, tomorrow, on our way back to Nigeria.' Jasmine informed Daba.

'Even Wilson you see there,' he said, pointing to the Ugandan, who covered his ears with a headphone.

'He has secured a scholarship with a university in California, USA. He too will be leaving any time soon. We have all made arrangements to leave this country,' he revealed.

'But don't worry,' he assured Daba and Victor.

'I will transfer you guys to another trusted agent, before we leave tomorrow,' he said, and went to cuddle Omon, who was still shaking from the previous incident.

***

'This time I want him dead, or alive,' was the verdict by Mallam Mahmud, after he received information about Jasmine's escape.

'You must have received the details on his new location by now. Have you?' the Mallam asked.

'Yes, father.' Hosni responded.

'Do not fail me this time,' the retired policeman said, and dismissed the boys.

***

The men with the two SUVs at Fatima's school a few days ago, had also received the coordinates to her new location. They were heading to her direction with full speed.

The squad was made up of loyalists of the overthrown Strongman of Libya. They are known as THE GREEN REVOLUTION. Their actual target was Mifta Rajab, who was one of the secret sponsors behind the overthrow, and killing of their idol Muammar Gaddafi, in 2011.

They desperately wanted to capture Fatima, to be a step closer to her elusive father.

***

'It's 10:58am.' Jasmine alerted his friends and Fatima.

'Let us go.' He said.

Wilson had earlier left the motel. He had been with Jasmine since the day before, and had to return home to get some stuff and then, go underground in Libya.

After a few minutes into their drive to the airport, Jasmine noticed a speeding red Audi, rushing towards them. He remembered the car from the beach, where he was attacked earlier.

'Do you see that?' Daba also noticed from the passenger's seat.

'Yes, I see them.' Jasmine replied and increased his speed.

"Pop-pop-pop."

"Rat-a-tat-tat."

Hosni and Yusuf fired from their Beretta 92G, given to them by their father, as two others with AK-47, shot from the back seat.

Other vehicles gave way to allow the Land Cruiser, and the Audi right of way, to avoid their crazy driving.

Suddenly, Jasmine felt a sharp pain, deep down his spin, and it was like the back of his left arm had just exploded. He lost control of the vehicle for a moment, which took the driver of the red car behind him by surprise, and he collided the Audi into the SUV, at full speed.

The force from the impact of the collision further destabilized Jasmine, who lost control of the vehicle. The car rushed onto a hill violently, and it turned over.

More than ten seconds passed, before anyone flinched a muscle inside the SUV, which was now upside down.

On the other side of the road, one of the assailants slowly came out of the badly damaged Audi, a few meters away. He frantically flagged down other vehicles, for someone to come to the aid of his colleagues, who were still trapped inside the car. Occasionally, he took a shot at the summersaulted SUV, with their target still inside.

It was the sound from the impact of the bullets on the body of the car that woke up those inside it.

Jasmine regained consciousness to the sight of blood dripping from his left hand, to the roof of the car. And it took him a few more seconds to recollect himself in the awkward position. He managed to take off his seat belt just as Daba arrived to assist him out of the car. He had also done the same for Fatima and Omon, while Victor had just set himself loose from a jammed seatbelt, and was now out of the car.

Ahead, they saw two black SUVs rushing from the distance to where they were. And it began to rain bullets yet again, as soon as the new assailants sighted their target, and the people around her by the hillside. This set came with even more sophisticated weapons.

"Rat-a-tat-tat." They fired from afar, as they approached the scene.

'Aargh!'Daba screamed, as he took a bullet to his right thigh, and he fell down flat. The others quickly went to the ground, and laid on all fours to dodge the bullets.

Jasmine for a moment thought the end has come, as he dragged himself a little closer to where Omon was, to cover her with his body. And the bullets kept on raining, as the Green Revolution militiamen got closer.

Then a chopper appeared from nowhere, and made to land at a flat surface, close to where Fatima and the others were.

They looked towards the aircraft and sighted someone armed with a rifle by the entrance of the helicopter. He enthusiastically waved at them to come on board.

Jasmine and Omon who were closest to the chopper, got to it first. But he turned around again and went to save his best friend Daba, who was struggling to join them, not too far behind.

He got to where Daba was, picked him off his feet and unto his right shoulder and made for the aircraft, while Victor and Fatima followed suit.

At that moment the SUVs came within view and the occupants disembarked from it speedily. That was when the man at the helicopter opened fire, and all hell was let loose as the sound of gunshot rattled the air, combined with the shrieking cry of the militiamen as they fired back.

Like in a slow motion scene in a John Woo movie, Jasmine took another bullet and felt another extremely hot sensation. This time, at the back of his right thigh, followed by a tremendous pain in that area of his leg. He fell to the ground, with Daba landing on top of him like a log.

At this point they both lay tummy to the ground, as bullets continued to rain in the air. But more of the noise was now coming from the direction of the chopper, whose gunner fired from a vantage position. Within minutes his big gun had silenced those from the opposite direction. Finally, the gun duel came to a halt. The man shooting from the red car and the occupants of the SUVs had either taken cover, or sustained fatal injuries. Suddenly it was all over.

Daba and Jasmine who had both sustained bullet wounds, began to crawl towards the chopper and were in desperate need of help. The noise from the exchange of fire had temporarily deafened them. They watched Victor help Fatima get on board and was springing back for them. He was accompanied by the gunner, who assisted in helping the wounded unto the waiting helicopter.

They got out of harm's way when the craft took to the skies, but not without taking some shots itself, as one determined fighter came out of his cover and gave it his last shot.

CHAPTER 18

THE GHOST IS BUSTED

Agent Jake Thomas stretched a dossier he was reading at the front seat of the police car, and interchanged his attention between the road and the vital document. He was leading a convoy to the Mitiga International Airport, to apprehend the suspect.

Contained in the document are details about John Mountbatten, otherwise known as Mifta Rajab. It had information from the day he was born, to his brilliant, but leftist articles as a young journalist.

Not since the Charismas of '89 when he was gifted a book titled: "The Adventures of Santa Clause" was Jake eager to consume something on prints so badly.

The data had just arrived from the Central Intelligence Agency's office in Madrid, Spain. And he could not wait to consume the information therein.

He has finally got good intelligence on the Britton, and what he is discovering was astonishing. The information made his chase after Jasmine seem like a waste of time, but he still wanted to apprehend the Chief of the MIEN all the same.

The transcript contained pictures and intelligence regarding John's current location at a fortress in Misratah. The mansion where he was hiding was owned by SALIM MOHAMMED, the son of Hamuz Mohammed, erstwhile leader of the Redeemers. He was the only surviving heir and patriarch of the Mohammed family. He was also now the leader of the New Redeemers, currently the strongest militia group in northern Libya.

Salim Mohammed was an untouchable in Libya, and it was he who was the prime source of Mifta Rajab's influence in the country.

John's relationship with his Boss's son Salim, had ensured the smooth running of his businesses, especially when he abandoned human trafficking and other small time hustling and became a full-time arms dealer. Thus he had maintained his original source of power in the country.

Together as partners, Salim Mohammed and Mifta Rajab had established the Clique, which has become a sophisticated and influential non-state actor.

They were now the major supplier of arms and ammunition to the opposition, in the conflict in Syria. Also, with the crisis in Libya, and in parts of the West African Chad basin, business was at its peak for John Mountbatten. The witty Briton had indeed gone into bigger things.

Jake now understood why he had been on the trail of the members of the nefarious organization without much success over the years.

To arrest John Mountbatten from such a fortress would be a matter for another day, he thought. But right now, he has to get Jasmine and Fatima at the airport.

At that point his convoy reached the place where a shootout had just occurred and he saw the chopper took to the skies.

Jake took out his cell phone and dialed local authorities to inform them about the incident. All the while, he kept his gaze on the disappearing helicopter as he watched the suspects escape.

He thought a stooge like Jasmine doesn't just get a military helicopter with all those resources to rescue him.

'Maybe there is something we are still missing.' He imagined.

Like a predator that had miss-caught his prey, Jake took off his dark Ray Ban Wayfarer, and removed his attention from the fleeing helicopter. He has to return to their base for mission reassessment. But he kept his mind on Jasmine, wondering what he has become in the organization in the span of less than a decade.

CHAPTER 19

HOMECOMING

The chopper later landed at a location in Misratah, the Mediterranean coastal city. The fortress had in place different infrastructure, including a well-equipped private hospital. There Jasmine and Daba who had both been wounded were taken to for immediate treatment.

Jasmine woke up the following morning to see Omon by his side, and Daba in another bed adjacent to his. Fatima was there too. She and the great Mifta Rajab, both stood by his bedside.

'Boss, good morning' Jasmine greeted Mifta Rajab, when he saw him.

'Good morning, Jamin.' John Mountbatten responded with humor, calling Jasmine by his adopted name in Libya. The gesture made Jasmine to let out a little smile, despite the pains, as he laid on the bed.

The man has become emaciated since their last meeting, that Jasmine could hardly recognized him. 'Was he sick?' He thought.

'How are you feeling, Jasmine?' John asked.

'I feel like am born again, Boss.' Jasmine responded, using his eyes to go over the bandages, plasters and straps that held him to the bed.

Jasmine literarily worships the man, although he has had to sacrifice a good part of his conscience in the course of executing odd and dangerous jobs for him.

Moreover, the ugly tasks had become less frequent since he diversified into arms trading, providing warring parties in the region with military equipment. Thus, his contact with jasmine in recent times had also become rare.

This was even more so following the return of Salim Mohammed from asylum in Saudi Arabia, just before the Arab Spring in 2010.

Looking at his Boss now he understood better. Something was definitely troubling the Ghost of North Africa.

'I hope you get well soon.' John said, breaking a brief moment of silence.

'And, thank you for bringing my girl to safety.' He said to Jasmine who had one of his legs heavily casted and suspended, with a bandage on his left arm, too.

'And you too,' he said again, this time looking towards the direction of Daba.

'Where is Victor?' Daba used the opportunity to ask. He thought he had given them enough time to catch up.

'Your friend is with Walid, or should be crossing the Mediterranean Sea as we speak.

'Our network in Niger, also reported that your other friend, who got lost in the desert has been found. He should be back in Nigeria already.' John replied Daba.

'Meanwhile, you guys can go anywhere you want, as soon as you get better. For now, you should concentrate on doing just that.' He said.

The authorities had arrested Kharig in a major bust at the Spotlight, many RECOs and members of the Clique were also apprehended during the raid. The pressure was mounting on John Mountbatten from different directions. So he, Amira and Fatima were leaving the country to an unspecified location. He had also handsomely rewarded Jasmine and his friend for the success of their last mission together.

Fatima got close to Jasmine's bed and gave him a kiss on his forehead, as her own way of showing appreciation.

'Thank you,' she said, before taking the stretched hand of her father, and both of them left together.

***

A few weeks later, their plane landed at the Nnamdi Azikiwe International Airport in Abuja, Nigeria.

They were the last to disembark from the mid-sized Boeing 707 aircraft, with Omon in front, while Jasmine and Daba hopped along with their clutches.

The mood at the airport terminal that afternoon was electrifying. Everyone seemed excited and engaged in a conversation with one person, or another. There was hardly any taciturn passenger, a relative or employee at the airport that day.

Jasmine for a moment, started to think about how convenient the environment was to smuggle something onto an aircraft, and literally had to shake the thought out of his head.

It was only after they got out of the airport that they understood what the fuzz was all about. The results of the 2015 Presidential election in Nigeria had just been affirmed by the courts. The General had been confirmed as the winner over the incumbent president.

What caught their interest most was the sense of belief and hope, clearly written on the faces of the people. They celebrated the victory inside the airport terminal, and outside under the active sun. Some of them waved the winning party's flag and insignias, such as the native broom.

'What are we going to do now?' Daba shouted at the top of his voice, as they followed the jamboree.

Some residents of Abuja had by now laid siege to major roads around the airport, and made noise from virtually anything they could lay their hands on, such as sticks, metals and even car honks.

'Don't worry Dabs!' Jasmine responded to Daba's earlier remark, using a palm to cover his ear, as he spoke into it like a public address system.

'Remember, there is nothing we can't fix.' Jasmine said, and then threw a hand over Daba's shoulders, as they waited at the taxi hub. Omon had hailed a cab and they were about to get into it.

'You are under arrest, Jasmine.'

The statement was sudden, unexpected and came as a rude shock.

Jasmine turned around and saw Agent Jake Thomas of the INTERPOL, in company of personnel of the Nigeria Police Force.

The End

AUTHOR'S NOTE

Dear Reader.

Welcome to "The Sahara Obstacle," a journey that spans continents and delves into the lives of some young Nigerians grappling with the harsh realities of their homeland. As a journalist with the Federal Radio Corporation of Nigeria, I've drawn upon my experiences to craft a tale that reflects not just the aspirations of its characters, but also the challenges and triumphs of millions facing similar paths.

In this novel, I explored themes close to my heart – migration, friendship, and the relentless pursuit of dreams amidst adversity. From the bustling streets of Nigeria to the arid expanses of Niger Republic and the perilous terrain of Libya, the protagonists – Daba, D1, Victor, and Mena – embark on a daring quest across the Sahara Desert, driven by hope and bound by friendship.

Through their eyes, I invite you to witness the complexities of migration, the bound that sustains us, and the sacrifices made in pursuit of a better future. It's a narrative that speaks to the resilience of the human spirit and the universal quest for opportunity and belonging.

I hope you find "The Sahara Obstacle" not only a gripping story but also a reflection of our times – a tribute to the courage and determination of those who defy the odds.

Warm regards,

Oghenero Jonathan Eghweree
Author

A NOTE ABOUT THE AUTHOR

Oghenero Jonathan Eghweree, is a Nigerian author and journalist with a career spanning over a decade with the Federal Radio Corporation of Nigeria (FRCN), where he currently serves as Principal Reporter|Editor. He holds a B.A. in International Studies and Diplomacy from the University of Benen, Benin City Nigeria, and a PGD in Mass Communication from the National Open University of Nigeria (NOUN). Oghenero is also the author of Muri the Whiz Rat.

DELIGHTFUL CLICKS DCSTUDIOS WED30042019

Also available by Oghenero Jonathan Eghweree

Muri The Whiz Rat

Muri the Whiz Rat tells the story of a courageous, super rat, who led its kind through a Lassa fever epidemic in Nigeria, against all odds.

WHAT READERS ARE SAYING

In Chapter 6, "The Sahara Obstacle," the author masterfully depicts the harsh reality of migration through the Sahara Desert. Victor's reflection of Africa's struggles, symbolized by the Sahara, is a powerful metaphor for the continent's challenges with nepotism, corruption, and the lack of opportunities that drive its youth to seek greener pastures abroad. The chapter vividly illustrates the perilous journey of Daba, Victor, Mena and D1, highlighting their courage, determination, and the tough choices they face in pursuit of a better life. It captures both the physical obstacles of the desert and the emotional toll of leaving one's homeland, emphasizing the resilience required to confront such a daunting journey.

MAXWELL AJUFO
Founder, Asaba Reading Club

This masterpiece of literary orchestra will practically get you fixated and overwhelmed with suspense as you anticipate the next twist or turn in its plots, exceptionally webbed and presented to give the reader an experience of the harrow journey through the Sahara Desert in the hope for a greener pasture in Europe, mostly forced upon many young Africans by the political and economic maladies on the continent. This a must read for all that care and seek the good for our beloved Africa.

JOLLY OKOOZA

Compelling read... exposes the dangers the youth confront to escape effects of corruption and bad leadership. Highly recommended.

HENRY ONOVWEGWHARE

The 'Sahara Obstacle' presents a gripping experience and tales of probably 'unwilling African migrants' fleeing unpleasant political and economic situation in Nigeria. In simple and plain language, it presents interesting and relatable story lines that leave readers bound. Oghenero Eghweree clearly demonstrates mastery of 'intriguing story telling'; weaving social, economic and political context to tell an amazing tale of obstacles faced by determined African migrants seeking better life outside the mother-land. This did not only reveal situations of 'unhinged migrants' united in their quest for better life by escaping bad governance and perilous economic situation in Nigeria, but jaw-dropping account of 'determined love-birds' also escaping parental disapproval to find peaceful clime to tie nuptial knot. This 'hard-to-drop' novel, describes the perilous journey by African migrants with graphic account of obstacles that the Sahara Desert pose to their quest to seek better life opportunities in Europe or America. Simplicity of language, relatable scenes and ingenuity of uncommon ability to use cultural context to tell 'relatable story', made Sahara Obstacle' a 'must read'.

CHARLES OGHENERUONAH, E.

Ph.D (Exeter).

This thought provoking book. THE SAHARA OBSTACLE, is apt, vivid account of the African youth' desire to sojourn and become what they aspire outside the continent. It is a fictional fact and recommended to all relevant agencies as guide to suppress influenced urge for inglorious ventures.

ALBERT OGRAKA

Poet, author of Dance of the Locusts (A collection of Poems)

This is an engaging tale studded with intriguing characters, charged situations that prick your mind to think of.... "Why the risk?" Definitely a must read.

ELIOGU THELMA

Manager News and Current Affairs, NTA

In this Book, 'The Sahara Obstacle', the author gives a riveting insight into the story of many Nigerians who have to embark on economic migration in search of the proverbial Golden Fleece. The Book is a must read, especially for adventurous youths who may not be aware of some of the dangers involved in such journeys. The Author's grasp of the undercurrents and obstacles in the journey across the Sahara is fascinating and eye popping.

ALAMBO DATONYE

Journalist

This is very lucid for studies, and it will enrich the knowledge for academic prowess... I hereby recommend this for sound academic activities. Regards.

PRINCE DR. OWEN NOSAKHARE AKENZUA, PhD

www.ingramcontent.com/pod-product-compliance
Lightning Source LLC
LaVergne TN
LVHW090439160826
845672LV00019B/1305

* 9 7 8 9 7 8 7 6 6 1 9 0 1 *